FACTOTUM

Charles Bukowski

Introduction by Neeli Cherkovski

Published by Virgin Books 2009

2 4 6 8 10 9 7 5 3 1

First published in Great Britain in 1981 by W.H. Allen & Co. Ltd.
First published by Virgin Books Ltd in 1992

This edition first published in Great Britain in 2009 by
Virgin Books
Random House, 20 Vauxhall Bridge Road
London SW1V 2SA

www.virginbooks.com
www.rbooks.co.uk

Addresses for companies within The Random House Group Limited can be
found at: www.randomhouse.co.uk/offices.htm

The Random House Group Limited Reg. No. 954009

A CIP catalogue record for this book is available from the British Library

ISBN 9780753518151

The Random House Group Limited supports The Forest Stewardship
Council [FSC], the leading international forest certification organisation. All
our titles that are printed on Greenpeace approved FSC certified paper carry
the FSC logo.
Our paper procurement policy can be found at www.rbooks.co.uk/
environment

Mixed Sources
Product group from well-managed
forests and other controlled sources
www.fsc.org Cert no. TT-COC-2139
© 1996 Forest Stewardship Council

Typeset by TW Typesetting, Plymouth, Devon
Printed and bound in Great Britain by CPI Bookmarque, Croydon CR0 4TD

FACTOTUM

28 NOV 2019

Introduction

By Neeli Cherkovski

Factotum is a tone poem to a certain era in Bukowski's life. The book begins with the sardonic Henry Chinaski's arrival in New Orleans, just off a cross-country bus, road-weary and hungry. He's restless, sex-starved, non-sentimental, and seemingly wise to the pitfalls of American life. His sights at this point in his young life are set no higher than serving as a "factotum" – a guy who does any job that comes along. The fact that other men his age are serving overseas (it is World War Two) offers a subtle backdrop. Here is the ultimate outsider, prone to glorify the seamy precincts of whatever town he visits and to shun propriety. Chinaski will not fall off the brink of the world – we are given the sense that he is strong-willed and able to manage himself on the streets, in cheap lodgings, and in the chaos of finding work – but neither is he going to land in a reliable job. He survives on his own terms, and the reader may take comfort in his endurance, so much so that *Factotum* depends entirely on Chinaski's keen focus. He defines himself clearly: "I had a cardboard suitcase that was falling apart. It had once been black but the black coating had peeled off and yellow cardboard was exposed." Coming right at the beginning of the book, this detail sets the tone. Chinaski never lets go as he sees beyond the veneer of things. It is what keeps him going against the odds. As he recognises the desperation of others, whether a prostitute luring him to her room or a fellow worker on the edge, he dances through it all as the ultimate outsider. There is no philosophising, simply a retelling of what he has observed. The jobs seem to drop out of the sky and just as quickly disappear.

Fortunately, Chinaski has a fall-back. His parents remain in L.A. along with the clean air of the 1940s, the cosy stucco houses, the hot meals appearing on the dinner table at the same time each evening. Despite his father's harshness and his mother's acquiescence to it, there is a clear sense that he has a home to go back to, taking some of the edge off his drifting around. In real life, Bukowski, the kid from Southern California, will return home after many false starts in other locales. The Chinaski of *Factotum* is Bukowski himself, a young man on a quest for self-definition. L.A. will serve as the capitol of his defiance against the status quo, while, at the same time, offering the solace of familiarity. It remains as a perpetual source. Those road trips sketched in Bukowski's autobiographical fiction (and in the real world) lasted only months at a time. The pull of the L.A. Basin was too strong, and his sense of place too lasting for things to be otherwise. Over the years, in interviews and in one-on-one conversation, Bukowski spoke of Los Angeles as a mistake and a national joke. Yet, toward the end of his life, in a rare moment of openness, he dubbed it "a spiritual city". To those who know his poetry and prose well, that should not come as a surprise. It had to do with those things he rarely mentions in his writing: the awesome sunsets, the tall palm trees lining the avenues like stately mandarins, the ripple of the Hollywood Hills, and the patchwork of neighbourhoods sprawling over hundreds of square miles. If he can show his own foibles in his work on the page, and glory in them, he is able to do the same with the terrain he came of age in, and in which he eventually prospered as a writer.

The lean prose and episodic nature of *Factotum* are suffused with sepia-toned portraits of a bygone era. The novel describes short-term jobs and the businesses where Chinaski/Bukowski tried his luck. It makes for a humorous necklace of words: lighting companies, bicycle warehouses, brake manufacturers, and the like. Los Angeles becomes a perverse opportunity for underemployment and scrutiny by tough supervisors eager to hand out a pink slip, shady characters in low-class bars and Bukowski himself, in the guise of Henry Chinaski, trying to find his place, living on and off with his girlfriend Jan (Jane Cooney Baker in real life). The mood is kept curiously light-hearted as each episode reveals successive snapshots of a young man making barely enough money for rent, let alone for a solid plate of food. He is able to laugh at his own predicament, accept himself as a fall guy, and not let others judge his intrinsic sense of self-worth. One sees this in Bukowski's poetry, a man who rises above the problems of daily life to stand in a terrain of his own design. In one great poem on Los Angeles he writes, "This land, punched-in, cuffed-out, divided, held like a crucifix in a death-hand . . . I walk on it, live on it a little while near Hollywood here."

Henry Chinaski is in fear of society because he feels betrayed by its mores. His defence against the status quo is to pre-judge, to accept defeat and to make of it a jumping-off point for further movement. There can be progress, but it is guarded. The reader is taken to a place where standard values are questioned, even those of the working class itself. At the same time, Bukowski extols self-reliance, originality and hard work. The literary rebel in him cannot quite shake off those classic American values. His most robust writing comes when he accepts the fact that he is giving voice to so many who struggle to subsist economically, while, at the same time, looking for meaning.

Bukowski had a yearning to write with the same relentless self-excoriation as Louis-Ferdinand Céline or Samuel Beckett, but he was trapped forever within the boundaries of American values. The darkness of Franz Kafka was a touch he admired: how to emulate the horror of Gregor Samsa, changing into an insect? It was only a notion he could keep at a distance. He was so attracted to the negations of Dostoevsky's hero in *Notes from the Underground* that he often pointed to his existential grumbling, which gives no quarter to convention, and lashes out at all values. He often said of that fictional character, "It's difficult to believe he was a literary invention. When I read *Notes* that negative force leapt off the pages and spoke my language." Despite such a close encounter, Bukowski's humour and mid-American belief system held sway. He could write about those on the bottom of society or on the margins, but with a light touch. We once argued over whether or not he had grown up in the middle class. I posited that despite his mocking of Henry Sr.'s touting of the work ethic, he lived it very well in his middle years. "You've got a point there," he admitted, and went on to say that you never wholly leave your roots. If he moved from town to town, state to state, and one employment opportunity to another at a fast-paced clip, it is what many young men of his generation did, especially those who feared the idea of settling down.

In its brevity and non-linearity, *Factotum* is a scrapbook of the author's past. It was written at speed. Bukowski challenged himself to, in his own words, "Get the job done as if I were sitting across the room talking to you." The episodes are helter-skelter. Some are only two or three pages in length. They constitute an anti-novel, rich in amusing characters you can visualise, even if Bukowski doesn't describe them in detail. It is the edge on which they survive, hanging on to illusion, lost in small-time labour and serving a boss, either present or hidden behind an office door. One may imagine the geography as being very different to what it is today. The freeways did not yet exist, except in a few places, rail and bus services were the major mode of inter-city travel, and a small-town atmosphere pervaded even such a major population centre as Los Angeles. Hollywood was still Hollywood, a real locale where actors and their agents, producers and directors burrowed into fancy bungalows on the hillside of the city. Citizens like Bukowski's father still believed you could make it through hard work and plain old endurance. Added to that, this was a land of geranium bushes, rose gardens, and small stucco courts where guys like the fictional Henry Chinaski dreamed of making it somehow. *Factotum* is set there, right in the middle of the town.

Bukowski's major themes – the battle of the sexes, the looming figure of the boss who goes strictly by the rulebook, the unfeeling parents, the demanding landlord – populate *Factotum*. There are the trademark Bukowski sex scenes, all laced with hard language, and the sense of distancing himself from intimacy. His stand-in Chinaski is forever on the existential journey, leaving little room for anyone else. The book ends with our hero sitting in a strip joint, somewhere in a muted corner of the vast metropolis, a keen and subdued observer: "Darlene danced over and grabbed the stage curtain. The curtain was torn and thick with dust. She grabbed it, dancing to the beat of the four man band and in the light of the pink spotlight." It is filmic and touching, a small detail of the larger picture, indelibly nailed to a time and period now museum-like. The old L.A. of *Factotum* is mythic in many minds. It is a newer place relatively, that grew old fast. Bukowski is the one to snag it and give it a touch of ordinary panache.

For John & Barbara Martin

The novelist does not long to see the lion eat grass. He realizes that one and the same God created the wolf and the lamb, then smiled, "seeing that his work was good."

– André Gide

1

I ARRIVED IN New Orleans in the rain at 5 o'clock in the morning. I sat around in the bus station for a while but the people depressed me so I took my suitcase and went out in the rain and began walking. I didn't know where the rooming houses were, where the poor section was.

I had a cardboard suitcase that was falling apart. It had once been black but the black coating had peeled off and yellow cardboard was exposed. I had tried to solve that by putting black shoepolish over the exposed cardboard. As I walked along in the rain the shoepolish on the suitcase ran and unwittingly I rubbed black streaks on both legs of my pants as I switched the suitcase from hand to hand.

Well, it was a new town. Maybe I'd get lucky.

The rain stopped and the sun came out. I was in the black district. I walked along slowly.

"Hey, poor white trash!"

I put my suitcase down. A high yellow was sitting on the porch steps swinging her legs. She did look good.

"Hello, poor white trash!"

I didn't say anything. I just stood there looking at her.

"How'd you like a piece of ass, poor white trash?"

She laughed at me. She had her legs crossed high and she kicked her feet; she had nice legs, high heels, and she kicked her legs and laughed. I picked up my suitcase and began to approach her up the walk. As I did I noticed a side curtain on a window to my left move just a bit. I saw a black man's face. He looked like Jersey Joe Wolcott. I backed down the pathway to the sidewalk. Her laughter followed me down the street.

2

I WAS IN a room on the second floor across from a bar. The bar was called The Gangplank Cafe. From my room I could see through the open bar doors and into the bar. There were some rough faces in that bar, some interesting faces. I stayed in my room at night and drank wine and looked at the faces in the bar while my money ran out. In the daytime I took long slow walks. I sat for hours staring at pigeons. I only ate one meal a day so my money would last longer. I found a dirty cafe with a dirty proprietor, but you got a big breakfast—hotcakes, grits, sausage—for very little.

3

I WENT OUT on the street, as usual, one day and strolled along. I felt happy and relaxed. The sun was just right. Mellow. There was peace in the air. As I approached the center of the block there was a man standing outside the doorway of a shop. I walked past.

"Hey, BUDDY!"

I stopped and turned.

"You want a job?"

I walked back to where he stood. Over his shoulder I could see a large dark room. There was a long table with men and women standing on both sides of it. They had hammers with which they pounded objects in front of them. In the gloom the objects appeared to be clams. They smelled like clams. I turned and continued walking down the street.

I remembered how my father used to come home each night and talk about his job to my mother. The job talk began when he entered the door, continued over the dinner table, and ended in the bedroom where my father would scream *"Lights Out!"* at 8 p.m., so he could get his rest and his full strength for the job the next day. There was no other subject except the job.

Down by the corner I was stopped by another man.

"Listen, my friend . . ." he began.

"Yes?" I asked.

"Listen, I'm a veteran of World War I. I put my life on the line for this country but nobody will hire me, nobody will give me a job. They don't appreciate what I did. I'm hungry, give me some help . . ."

"I'm not working."

"You're not working?"

"That's right."

I walked away. I crossed the street to the other side.

"You're lying!" he screamed. *"You're working. You've got a job!"*

A few days later I was looking for one.

4

HE WAS A man behind the desk with a hearing aid and the wire ran down along the side of his face and into his shirt where he hid the battery. The office was dark and comfortable. He was dressed in a worn brown suit with a wrinkled white shirt and a necktie frayed at the edges. His name was Heathercliff.

I had seen the ad in the local paper and the place was near my room.

Need ambitious young man with an eye to the future. Exper. not necessary. Begin in delivery room and work up.

I waited outside with five or six young men, all of them trying to look ambitious. We had filled out our employment applications and now we waited. I was the last to be called.

"Mr. Chinaski, what made you leave the railroad yards?"

"Well, I don't see any future in the railroads."

"They have good unions, medical care, retirement."

"At my age, retirement might almost be considered superfluous."

"Why did you come to New Orleans?"

"I had too many friends in Los Angeles, friends I felt were hindering my career. I wanted to go where I could concentrate unmolested."

"How do we know that you'll remain with us any length of time?"

"I might not."

"Why?"

"Your ad stated that there was a future for an ambitious man. If there isn't any future here then I must leave."

"Why haven't you shaved your face? Did you lose a bet?"

"Not yet."

"Not yet?"

"No; I bet my landlord that I could land a job in one day even with this beard."

"All right, we'll let you know."

"I don't have a phone."

"That's all right, Mr. Chinaski."

I left and went back to my room. I went down the dirty hall and took a hot bath. Then I put my clothes back on and went out and got a bottle of wine. I came back to the room and sat by the window drinking and watching the people in the bar, watching the people walk by. I drank slowly and began to think again of getting a gun and doing it quickly—without all the thought and talk. A matter of guts. I wondered about my guts. I finished the bottle and went to bed and slept. About 4 p.m. I was awakened by a knock on the door. It was a Western Union boy. I opened the telegram:

MR. H. CHINASKI. REPORT TO WORK 8 AM TOMORROW. R.M. HEATHER-CLIFF CO.

5

IT WAS A magazine publishers distributing house and we stood at the packing table checking the orders to see that the quantities coincided with the invoices. Then we signed the invoice and either packed the order for out of town shipment or set the magazines aside for local truck delivery. The work was easy and dull but the clerks were in a constant state of turmoil. They were worried about their jobs. There was a mixture of young men and women and there didn't seem to be a foreman. After several hours an argument began between two of the women. It was something about the magazines. We were packing comic books and something had gone wrong across the table. The two women became violent as the argument went on.

"Look," I said, "these books aren't worth reading let alone arguing about."

"All right," one of the women said, "we know you think you're too good for this job."

"Too good?"

"Yes, your attitude. You think we didn't notice it?"

That's when I first learned that it wasn't enough to just *do* your job, you had to have an interest in it, even a passion for it.

I worked there three or four days, then on Friday we were paid right up to the hour. We were given yellow envelopes with green bills and the exact change. Real money, no checks.

Toward quitting time the truck driver came back a little early. He sat on a pile of magazines and smoked a cigarette.

"Yeah, Harry," he said to one of the clerks, "I got a raise today. I got a two dollar raise."

At quitting time I stopped for a bottle of wine, went up to my room, had a drink then went downstairs and phoned my company. The phone rang a long time. Finally Mr. Heathercliff answered. He was still there.

"Mr. Heathercliff?"

"Yes?"

"This is Chinaski."

"Yes, Mr. Chinaski?"

"I want a two dollar raise."

"What?"

"That's right. The truck driver got a raise."

"But he's been with us two years."

"I need a raise."

"We're giving you seventeen dollars a week now and you're asking for nineteen?"

"That's right. Do I get it or not?"

"We just can't do it."

"Then I quit." I hung up.

6

MONDAY I WAS hungover. I shaved off my beard and followed up an ad. I sat across from the editor, a man in shirt sleeves with deep hollows under his eyes. He looked as if he hadn't slept for a week. It was cool and dark in there. It was the composing room of one of the town's two newspapers, the small one. Men sat at desks under reading lamps working at copy.

"Twelve dollars a week," he said.

"All right," I said, "I'll take it."

I worked with a little fat man with an unhealthy looking paunch. He had an old-fashioned pocket watch on a gold chain and he wore a vest, a green sunshade, had thick lips and a meaty dark look to his face. The lines in his face had no interest or character; his face looked as if it had been folded several times and then smoothed out, like a piece of cardboard. He wore square shoes and chewed tobacco, squirting the juice into a spitoon at his feet.

"Mr. Belger," he said of the man who needed the sleep, "has worked hard to put this paper on its feet. He's a good man. We were going bankrupt until he came along."

He looked at me. "They usually give this job to a college boy."

He's a frog, I thought, that's what he is.

"I mean," he said, "this job usually goes to a student. He can study his books while he waits for a call. Are you a student?"

"No."

"This job usually goes to a student."

I walked back to my work room and sat down. The room was filled with rows and rows of metal drawers and in the drawers were zinc engravings that had been used for ads. Many of these engravings were used again and again. There was also lots of type—customer names and logos. The fat man would scream "*Chinaski!*" and I'd go see which ad or what type he wanted. Often I was sent to the competing newspaper to borrow some of their type. They borrowed ours. It was a nice walk and I found a place in a back alley where I could get a glass of beer for a nickel. There weren't many calls from the fat man and the nickel beer place became my hangout. The fat man began to miss me. At first he simply gave me unkind looks. Then one day he asked:

"Where you been?"

"Out getting a beer."

"This is a job for a student."

"I'm not a student."

"I gotta let you go. I need somebody who is right here all the time available."

The fat man took me over to Belger who looked as tired as ever. "This is a job for a student, Mr. Belger. I'm afraid this man doesn't fit in. We need a student."

"All right," said Belger. The fat man padded off.

"What do we owe you?" asked Belger.

"Five days."

"O.K., take this down to payroll."

"Listen, Belger, that old fuck is disgusting."

Belger sighed. "Jesus Christ, don't I know it?"

I went down to payroll.

7

WE WERE STILL in Louisiana. The long train ride through Texas lay ahead. They gave us cans of food but no openers. I stored my cans on the floor and stretched out on the wooden seat. The other men were gathered in the front of the coach, sitting together, talking and laughing. I closed my eyes.

After about ten minutes I felt dust rising up through the cracks in the plank seat. It was very old dust, coffin dust, it stank of death, of something that had been dead for a long time. It filtered into my nostrils, settled into my eyebrows, tried to enter my mouth. Then I heard heavy breathing sounds. Through the cracks I could see a man crouched behind the seat, blowing the dust into my face. I sat up. The man scrambled out from behind the seat and ran to the front of the car. I wiped my face and stared at him. It was hard to believe.

"If he comes up here I want you fellows to help me," I heard him say. "You gotta promise to help me . . ."

The gang of them looked back at me. I stretched out on the seat again. I could hear them talking:

"What's wrong with him?" "Who does he think he is?" "He don't speak to nobody." "He just stays back there by himself."

"When we get him out there on those tracks we'll take care of him. The bastard."

"You think you can take him, Paul? He looks crazy to me."

"If I can't take him, somebody can. He'll eat shit before we're done."

Some time later I walked to the front of the car for a drink of water. As I walked by they stopped talking. They watched me in silence as I drank water from the cup. Then as I turned and walked back to my seat they started talking again.

The train made many stops, night and day. At every stop where there was a bit of green and a small town nearby, one or two of the men would jump off.

"Hey, what the hell happened to Collins and Martinez?"

The foreman would take his clipboard and cross them off the list. He walked back to me. "Who are you?"

"Chinaski."

"You staying with us?"

"I need the job."

"O.K." He walked away.

AT EL PASO the foreman came through and told us we were switching trains. We were given tickets good for one night at a nearby hotel and a meal ticket to use at a local cafe; also directions on how, when and where to board the next train through in the a.m.

I waited outside the cafe as the men ate and as they came out picking their teeth and talking, I walked in.

9

"We'll get his ass good, that son of a bitch!"

"Man, I hate that ugly bastard."

I went in and ordered a hamburger steak with onions and beans. There wasn't any butter for the bread but the coffee was good. When I came out they were gone. A bum was walking up the sidewalk toward me. I gave him my hotel ticket.

I slept in the park that night. It seemed safer. I was tired and that hard park bench didn't bother me at all. I slept.

Some time later I was awakened by what sounded like a roar. I never knew that alligators roared. Or more exactly it was many things: a roar, an agitated inhale, and a hiss. I also heard the snapping of jaws. A drunken sailor was in the center of the pond and he had one of the alligators by the tail. The creature tried to twist and reach the sailor but found it difficult. The jaws were horrifying but very slow and uncoordinated. Another sailor and a young girl stood watching and laughing. Then the sailor kissed the girl and they walked off together leaving the other fighting the alligator . . .

I was next awakened by the sun. My shirt was hot. It was almost burning. The sailor was gone. So was the alligator. On a bench to the east sat a girl and two young men. They had evidently slept in the park that night too. One of the young men stood up.

"Mickey," said the young girl, "you've got a hard-on!"

They laughed.

"How much money we got?"

They looked through their pockets. They had a nickel.

"Well, what are we going to do?"

"I don't know. Let's start walking."

I watched them walk off, out of the park, into the city.

8

WHEN THE TRAIN stopped in Los Angeles we had a two or three day stopover. They issued hotel and meal tickets again. I gave my hotel tickets to the first bum I met. As I was walking along looking for the cafe where I would use my meal tickets I found myself behind two of the men who had shared the ride from New Orleans. I walked faster until I was alongside of them.

"How are you doing fellows?" I asked.

"Oh, everything's all right, everything's fine."

"Are you sure? Nothing bothering you?"

"No, everything's all right."

I went ahead and found the cafe. They served beer there so I exchanged my tickets for beer. The whole track gang was there. When I'd used up my tickets I had just enough change to take a streetcar back to the home of my parents.

9

MY MOTHER SCREAMED when she opened the door. "*Son! Is that you, son?*"

"I need some sleep."

"Your bedroom is always waiting."

I went to the bedroom, undressed and climbed into bed. I was awakened about 6 p.m. by my mother. "Your father is home."

I got up and began to dress. Dinner was on the table when I walked in.

My father was a big man, taller than I was with brown eyes; mine were green. His nose was too large and you couldn't help noticing his ears. His ears wanted to leap away from his head.

"Listen," he said, "if you stay here I am going to charge you room and board plus laundry. When you get a job, what you owe us will be subtracted from your salary until you are paid up."

We ate in silence.

10

MY MOTHER HAD found a job. She was to start the next day. This left the house to me. After breakfast and after my parents had left for their jobs I took off my clothes and went back to bed. I masturbated and then made a time study in an old school notebook of the airplanes passing overhead. I decorated the time study with some pleasantly obscene drawings. I knew that my father would charge me atrocious prices for room, board and laundry and that he would also be careful to list me as a dependent on his income tax return, but the desire to find a job did not seem to be with me.

As I relaxed in bed I had this strange feeling in my head. It was as if my skull was made of cotton, or was a small balloon filled with air. I could feel *space* in my skull. I couldn't comprehend it. Soon I stopped wondering about it. I was comfortable, it wasn't agonizing. I listened to symphony music, smoking my father's cigarettes.

I got up and walked into the front room. In the house across the street was a young wife. She had on a short tight brown dress. She sat on the steps of her house which was directly across the street. I could look well up her dress. I watched from behind the drapes of the front window, looking up her dress. I became excited. Finally I masturbated again. I bathed and dressed and sat about smoking more cigarettes. About 5 p.m. I left the house and went for a long walk, walking for almost an hour.

When I returned, both of my parents were home. Dinner was about ready. I went to my bedroom and waited to be called. I was called. I went in.

"Well," said my father, "did you find a job?"

"No."

"Listen, any man who wants work can find work."

"Maybe so."

"I can hardly believe you're my son. You don't have any ambition, you don't have any get-up-and-go. How the hell are you going to make it in this world?"

He put a number of peas into his mouth and spoke again: "What's this cigarette smoke in here? *Pooh!* I had to open all the windows! The air was *blue*!"

11

THE NEXT DAY I went back to bed for a while after they were gone. Then I got up and went to the front room and looked out between the drapes. The young housewife was again sitting on her steps across the street. She had on a different, sexier dress. I looked at her a long time. Then I masturbated slowly and at leisure.

I bathed and dressed. I found some empty bottles in the kitchen and cashed them in at the grocery. I found a bar on the Avenue and went in and ordered a draft beer. There were a great many drunks in there playing the juke box, talking loudly and laughing. Now and then a new beer arrived in front of me. Somebody was buying. I drank. I began talking to people.

Then I looked outside. It was evening, almost dark. The beers kept arriving. The fat woman who owned the bar and her boyfriend were friendly.

I went outside once to fight somebody. It wasn't a good fight. We were both too drunk and there were large potholes in the asphalt surface of the parking lot that made our footing difficult. We quit . . .

* * *

I AWAKENED much later in an upholstered red booth at the back of the bar. I got up and looked around. Everybody was gone. The clock said 3:15. I tried the door, it was locked. I went behind the bar and got myself a bottle of beer, opened it, came back and sat down. Then I went and got myself a cigar and a bag of chips. I finished my beer, got up and found a bottle of vodka, one of scotch and sat down again. I mixed them with water; I smoked cigars, and ate beef jerky, chips, and hard-boiled eggs.

I drank until 5 a.m. I cleaned the bar then, put everything away, went to the door, let myself out. As I did I saw a police car approach. They drove along slowly behind me as I walked.

After a block they pulled up alongside. An officer stuck his head out. "Hey, buddy!"

Their lights were in my face.

"What are you doing?"

"Going home."

"You live around here?"

"Yes."

"Where?"

"2122 Longwood Avenue."

"What were you doing coming out of that bar?"

"I'm the janitor."

"Who owns that bar?"

"A lady named Jewel."

"Get in."

I did.

"Show us where you live."

They drove me home.

"Now, get out and ring the bell."

I walked up the drive. I went up on the porch, rang the bell. There was no answer.

I rang again, several times. Finally the door opened. My mother and father stood there in their pajamas and robes.

"*You're drunk!*" my father screamed.

"Yes."

"Where do you get the money to drink? You don't have any money!"

"I'll get a job."

"*You're drunk! You're drunk! My Son is a Drunk! My Son is a God Damned No-Good Drunk!*"

The hair on my father's head was standing up in crazy tufts. His eyebrows were wild, his face puffed and flushed with sleep.

"You act as if I had murdered somebody."

"*It's just as bad!*"

". . . ooh, shit . . ."

Suddenly I vomited on their Persian *Tree of Life* rug. My mother screamed. My father lunged toward me.

"Do you know what we do to a dog when he shits on the rug?"

"Yes."

He grabbed the back of my neck. He pressed down, forcing me to bend at the waist. He was trying to force me to my knees.

"I'll show you."

"Don't . . ."

My face was almost into it.

"I'll show you what we do to dogs!"

I came up from the floor with the punch. It was a perfect shot. He staggered back all the way across the room and sat down on the couch. I followed him over.

"Get up."

He sat there. I heard my mother. "*You Hit Your Father! You Hit Your Father! You Hit Your Father!*"

She screamed and ripped open one side of my face with her fingernails.

"Get up," I told my father.

"*You Hit Your Father!*"

She scratched my face again. I turned to look at her. She got the other side of my face. Blood was running down my neck, was soaking my shirt, pants, shoes, the rug. She lowered her hands and stared at me.

"Have you finished?"

She didn't answer. I walked back to the bedroom thinking, I better find myself a job.

12

I STAYED IN my room until after they left the next morning. Then I took the newspaper and turned to the Help Wanted section. My face hurt; I was still sick. I circled some ads, shaved as best I could, took a few aspirin, dressed, and walked over to the Boulevard. I put my thumb out. The cars went by. Then a car stopped. I got in.

"Hank!"

It was an old friend, Timmy Hunter. We'd gone to Los Angeles City College together.

"What are you doing, Hank?"

"Looking for a job."

"I'm going to Southern Cal now. What happened to your face?"

"The fingernails of a woman."

"Yeh?"

"Yeh. Timmy, I need a drink."

Timmy parked at the next bar. We went in and he ordered two bottles of beer.

"What kind of job you looking for?"

"Stockboy, shipping clerk, janitor."

"Listen, I got some money at home. I know a good bar in Inglewood. We can go there."

He was living with his mother. We went in and the old

lady looked up from her newspaper: "Hank, don't you go getting Timmy drunk."

"How are you doing, Mrs. Hunter?"

"The last time you and Timmy went out you both ended up in jail."

Timmy put his books in the bedroom and came out. "Let's go," he said.

It was Hawaiian decor, crowded. A man was on the phone: "You got to have somebody come get the truck. I'm too drunk to drive. Yes, I know I've lost the goddamned job, just come and get the truck!"

Timmy bought, we both drank. His conversation was O.K. A young blonde was glancing over and showing me leg. Timmy talked on and on. He talked about City College: how we kept wine bottles in our locker; about Popoff and his wooden guns; about Popoff and his real guns; about how we shot the bottom out of a boat in Westlake Park and sank; about the time the students went on strike in the college gym . . .

The drinks kept coming. The young blonde girl left with someone else. The juke box played. Timmy talked on. It was getting dark. We were 86'd, walked down the street looking for another bar. It was 10 p.m. We could hardly stand up. The street was full of cars.

"Look Timmy, let's rest."

I saw it. A mortuary, like a colonial mansion, with floodlights, and a wide white staircase leading up to the porch.

Timmy and I went about halfway up the staircase. Then I carefully stretched him out on a step. I straightened his legs and put his arms neatly down by his sides. Then I stretched out in a similar position on the step below Timmy.

13

I woke up in a room. I was alone. It was just getting light. It was cold. I was in my shirtsleeves. I tried to think. I got up from the hard bunk, went to the window. It was barred. There was the Pacific Ocean. (Somehow I was in Malibu.) The jailor came along about an hour later, banging metal dishes and trays. He passed my breakfast through to me. I sat down and ate, listening to the ocean.

Forty-five minutes later I was taken outside. There was a gang of men standing handcuffed together on one long chain. I walked to the end and held out my hands. The guard said, "Not you." I got my own set of cuffs. Two officers put me in a squad car and we drove off.

We reached Culver City and parked in back of the courthouse. One of the policemen got out with me. We walked to the back way and sat down in the front row of the courtroom. The cop took the cuffs off. I didn't see Timmy anywhere. There was the usual long wait for the judge. My case was second.

"You are accused of public intoxication and of blocking traffic. Ten days or thirty dollars."

I pleaded guilty even though I didn't know what he meant about blocking traffic. The policeman took me downstairs, sat me in the back of the squad car. "You got off easy," he said. "You guys had traffic jammed up for a mile. It was the worst traffic jam in the history of the City of Inglewood."

Then he drove me to L.A. County Jail.

14

THAT NIGHT MY father arrived with the thirty dollars. As we left his eyes were moist. "You've disgraced your mother and myself," he said. It seemed they knew one of the policemen who had asked him, "Mr. Chinaski, what is *your* son doing here?"

"I was so ashamed. To think, my own son in prison."

We walked down to his car, got in. He drove off. He was still weeping. "It's bad enough you don't want to serve your country in time of War . . ."

"The shrink said I was unfit."

"My son, if it wasn't for the First World War I never would have met your mother and you never would have been born."

"Do you have a cigarette?"

"Now you've been jailed. A thing like this could kill your mother."

We passed some cheap bars on lower Broadway.

"Let's go in and catch a drink."

"What? You mean you'd dare drink right after getting out of jail for intoxication?"

"That's when you need a drink the most."

"Don't you ever tell your mother you wanted a drink right after getting out of jail," he warned me.

"I need a piece of ass too."

"What?"

"I said, I need a piece of ass too."

He nearly ran a red light. We drove in silence.

"By the way," he said finally, "I guess you know that the jail fine will be added to your room, board and laundry bill?"

15

I GOT A job in an auto parts warehouse just off Flower Street. The manager was a tall ugly man with no ass. He always told me whenever he fucked his wife the night before.

"I fucked my wife last night. Get that Williams Brothers order first."

"We're out of K-3 flanges."

"Backorder them."

I stamped "B.O." on the packing slip and invoice.

"I fucked my wife last night."

I taped up the Williams Brothers box, labeled it, weighed it, and affixed the necessary postage.

"It was pretty good too."

He had a sandy mustache, sandy hair and no ass.

"She pissed when she finished."

16

MY BILL FOR room, board, laundry, etc., was so high by this time that it took several paychecks to get even. I stayed until then and moved out right afterwards. I couldn't afford the rates at home.

I found a rooming house near my job. Moving wasn't hard. I only owned enough to half fill a suitcase . . .

MAMA STRADER was my landlady, a dyed redhead with a good figure, many gold teeth, and an aged boyfriend. She called me into the kitchen the first morning and said she'd pour me a whiskey if I would go out back and feed the chickens. I did and then I sat in the kitchen drinking with Mama and her boyfriend, Al. I was an hour late for work.

The second night there was a knock on my door. It was a fat woman in her mid-forties. She held a bottle of wine. "I live down the hall, my name's Martha. I hear you listening to that good music all the time. I thought I'd bring you a drink."

Martha walked in. She had on a loose green smock, and

after a few wines she started showing me her legs. "I've got good legs."

"I'm a leg man."

"Look higher."

Her legs were very white, fat, flabby, with bulging purple veins. Martha told me her story.

She was a whore. She made the bars off and on. Her main source of income was the owner of a department store. "He gives me money. I go into his store and take anything I want. The salespeople don't bother me. He's told them to leave me alone. He doesn't want his wife to know I'm a better fuck than she is."

Martha got up and turned on the radio. Loud. "I'm a good dancer," she said. "Watch me dance!"

She whirled in her green tent, kicking her legs. She wasn't so hot. Soon she had the smock up around her waist and was waving her behind in my face. The pink panties had a large hole over the right cheek. Then off came the smock and she was just in her panties. Next the panties were on the floor by the smock and she was doing a grind. Her triangle of cunt hair was almost hidden by her dangling, bouncing stomach.

Sweat was making her mascara run. Suddenly her eyes narrowed. I was sitting on the edge of the bed. She leapt on me before I could move. Her open mouth was pressed on mine. It tasted of spit and onions and stale wine and (I imagined) the sperm of four hundred men. She pushed her tongue into my mouth. It was thick with saliva, I gagged and pushed her off. She fell on her knees, tore open my zipper, and in a second my soft pecker was in her mouth. She sucked and bobbed. Martha had a small yellow ribbon in her short grey hair. There were warts and big brown moles on her neck and cheeks.

My penis rose; she groaned, bit me. I screamed, grabbed her by the hair, pulled her off. I stood in the center of the room wounded and terrified. They were playing a Mahler Symphony on the radio. Before I could move she was down on her knees and on me again. She gripped my balls mercilessly with both of her hands. Her mouth opened, she had me; her head bobbed, sucked, jerked. Giving my balls a tremendous yank while almost biting my pecker in half she forced me to the floor. Sucking sounds filled the room as my radio played Mahler. I felt as if I were being eaten by a pitiless animal. My pecker rose, covered with spittle and blood. The sight of it threw her into a frenzy. I felt as if I was being eaten alive.

If I come, I thought desperately, I'll never forgive myself.

As I reached down to try to yank her off by the hair, she clutched my balls again and squeezed them without pity. Her teeth scissored midpoint on my penis as if to slice me in two. I screamed, let go of her hair, fell back. Her head bobbed remorselessly. I was certain the sucking could be heard all over the roominghouse.

"NO!" I yelled.

She persisted with inhuman fury. I began to come. It was like sucking the insides out of a trapped snake. Her fury was mixed with madness; she sucked at that sperm, gurgling it into her throat.

She continued to bob and suck.

"Martha! Stop! It's over!"

She wouldn't. It was as if she had been turned into an enormous all-devouring mouth. She continued to suck and bob. She went on, on. "NO!" I yelled again ... This time she got it like a vanilla malt through a straw.

I collapsed. She rose and began dressing herself. She sang.

*"When a New York baby says goodnight
it's early in the morning*

goodnight, sweetheart
it's early in the morning

goodnight, sweetheart
milkman's on his way home . . ."

I staggered to my feet, clutching the front of my pants and found my wallet. I took out $5, handed it to her. She took the $5, tucked it into the front of her dress between her breasts, grabbed my balls playfully once again, squeezed, let go, and waltzed out of the room.

17

I HAD WORKED long enough to save up bus fare to somewhere else, plus a few dollars to take care of me after I arrived. I quit my job, took out a map of the United States and looked it over. I decided on New York City.

I took five pints of whiskey in my suitcase on the bus with me. Whenever somebody sat next to me and began talking I pulled out a pint and took a long drink. I got there.

The bus station in New York City was near Times Square. I walked out into the street with my old suitcase. It was evening. The people swarmed up out of the subways. Like insects, faceless, mad, they rushed upon me, into and around me, with much intensity. They spun and pushed each other; they made horrible sounds.

I stood back in a doorway and finished the last pint.

Then I walked along, pushed, elbowed, until I saw a vacancy sign on Third Avenue. The manager was an old Jewish woman. "I need a room," I told her.

"You need a good suit, my boy."

"I'm broke."

"It's a good suit, almost for nothing. My husband runs the tailor shop across the street. Come with me."

I paid for my room, put my suitcase upstairs. I went with her across the street.

"Herman, show this boy the suit."

"Ah, it's a nice suit." Herman brought it out; a dark blue, a bit worn.

"It looks too small."

"No, no, it fits good."

He came out from behind the counter with the suit. "Here. Try the coat on." Herman helped me into it. "See? It fits . . . You want to try the pants?" He held the pants in front of me, from waist to toe.

"They look all right."

"Ten dollars."

"I'm broke."

"Seven dollars."

I gave Herman the seven dollars, took my suit upstairs to my room. I went out for a bottle of wine. When I got back I locked the door, undressed, made ready for my first real night's sleep in some time.

I got into bed, opened the bottle, worked the pillow into a hard knot behind my back, took a deep breath, and sat in the dark looking out of the window. It was the first time I had been alone for five days. I was a man who thrived on solitude; without it I was like another man without food or water. Each day without solitude weakened me. I took no pride in my solitude; but I was dependent on it. The darkness of the room was like sunlight to me. I took a drink of wine.

Suddenly the room filled with light. There was a clatter and a roar. The El ran level with the window of my room. A subway train had stopped there. I looked out into a row of New York faces who looked back. The train lingered, then pulled away. It was dark. Then the room filled again with light. Again I looked into the faces. It was like a vision of hell repeated again and again. Each new trainload of faces was more ugly, demented and cruel than the last. I drank the wine.

It continued: darkness, then light; light, then darkness. I finished the wine and went out for more. I came back, undressed, got back in bed. The arrival and departure of the faces continued; I felt I was having a vision. I was being visited by hundreds of devils that the Devil Himself couldn't tolerate. I drank more wine.

Finally I got up and took my new suit out of the closet. I slipped into the coat. It was a tight fit. The coat seemed smaller than when I was in the tailor shop. Suddenly there was a ripping sound. The coat had split open straight up the back. I took what remained of the coat off. I still had the pants. I worked my legs into them. There were buttons in the front instead of a zipper; as I tried to fasten them, the seam split in the seat. I reached in from behind and felt my shorts.

18

FOR FOUR OR five days I walked around. Then I got drunk for two days. I moved out of my room and into Greenwich Village. One day I read in Walter Winchell's column that O. Henry used to do all of his writing at a table in some famous writers' bar. I found the bar and went in looking for what?

It was noon. I was the only patron despite Winchell's column. There I stood alone with a large mirror, the bar, and the bartender.

"I'm sorry, sir, we can't serve you."

I was stunned, couldn't answer. I waited for an explanation.

"You're drunk."

I was probably hungover but I hadn't had a drink for twelve hours. I mumbled something about O. Henry and left.

19

IT LOOKED LIKE a deserted store. There was a sign in the window: *Help Wanted*. I went in. A man with a thin mustache smiled at me. "Sit down." He gave me a pen and a form. I filled out the form.

"Ah? College?"

"Not exactly."

"We're in advertising."

"Oh?"

"Not interested?"

"Well, you see, I've been painting. A *painter*, you know? I've run out of money. Can't sell the stuff."

"We get lots of those."

"I don't like them either."

"Cheer up. Maybe you'll be famous after you're dead."

He went on to say the job entailed night work to begin with, but that there was always a chance to work one's way up.

I told him that I liked night work. He said that I could begin in the subway.

20

TWO OLD GUYS were waiting for me. I met them down inside the subway where the cars were parked. I was given an armful of cardboard posters and a small metal instrument that looked like a can opener. We all climbed in one of the parked cars.

"Watch me," one of the old guys said.

He jumped up on the dusty seats, began walking along ripping out old posters with his can opener. So that's how those things get up there, I thought. People put them there.

Each poster was held by two metal strips which had to be removed to get the new poster in. The strips were spring-tight and curved to fit the contour of the wall.

They let me try it. The metal strips resisted my efforts. They wouldn't budge. The sharp edges cut my hands as I worked. I began to bleed. For each poster you took out there was a new poster to replace it. Each one took forever. It was endless.

"There are green bugs all over New York," said one of the old guys after a while.

"There are?"

"Yeh. You new in New York?"

"Yes."

"Don't you know all New York people got these green bugs?"

"No."

"Yeh. Woman wanted to fuck me last night. I said, 'No, baby, nothing doing.'"

"Yeh?"

"Yeh. I told her I'd do it if she gave me five bucks. It takes five bucks worth of steak to replace that jizz."

"She give you the five bucks?"

"Nah. She offered me a can of Campbell's mushroom soup."

We worked our way down to the end of the car. The two old men climbed off the back, began to walk toward the next subway car parked about fifty feet up the track. We were forty feet above the ground with nothing but railroad ties to walk on. I saw it wouldn't be any trouble at all for a body to slip through and fall to the ground below.

I climbed out of the subway car and slowly started stepping from tie to tie, can opener in one hand, cardboard posters in the other. A subway car filled with passengers pulled up; the lights from the train showed the way.

The train moved off; I was in total darkness. I could neither see the ties nor the spaces between them. I waited.

The two old guys hollered from the next car: "Come on! Hurry! We got a lot of work to do!"

"Wait! I can't see!"

"We ain't got all night!"

My eyes began to adjust. Step by step I went forward, slowly. When I reached the next car I put the posters on the floor and sat down. My legs were weak.

"What's the matter?"

"I don't know."

"What is it?"

"A man can get killed up here."

"Nobody's ever fallen through yet."

"I feel like I could."

"It's all in the mind."

"I know. How do I get out of here?"

"There's a stairway right over there. But you gotta cross a lotta tracks, you gotta watch for trains."

"Yes."

"And don't step on the third rail."

"What's that?"

"That's the power. It's the gold rail. It looks like gold. You'll see it."

I got down on the tracks and began stepping over them. The two old men watched me. The gold rail was there. I stepped very high over that.

Then I half-ran half-fell down the stairway. There was a bar across the street.

21

THE HOURS AT the dog biscuit factory were from 4:30 p.m. to 1 a.m.

I was given a dirty white apron and heavy canvas gloves. The gloves were burned and had holes in them. I could see my fingers peeking through. I was given instructions by a toothless elf with a film over his left eye; the film was white-and-green with spidery blue lines.

He had been on the job nineteen years.

I advanced to my post. A whistle blew and the machinery leaped into action. Dog biscuits began to move. The dough was stamped into shape and then placed on heavy metal screens with iron edges.

I grabbed a screen, placed it in the oven behind me. I turned. There was the next screen. There was no way to slow them down. The only time they stopped was when something snagged the machinery. It didn't happen often. When it did, the Elf got it going quickly.

The flames of the oven leaped fifteen feet high. The inside of the oven was like a ferris wheel. Each ledge held twelve screens. When the oven man (me) had filled a ledge he kicked a lever which turned the wheel one notch, bringing down the next empty ledge.

The screens were heavy. Lifting one screen could tire a man. If you thought about doing it for eight hours, lifting hundreds of screens, you'd never make it. Green biscuits, red biscuits, yellow biscuits, brown biscuits, purple biscuits, blue biscuits, vitamin biscuits, vegetable biscuits.

On such jobs men become tired. They experience a weariness beyond fatigue. They say mad, brilliant things. Out of my head, I cussed and talked and cracked jokes and sang. Hell boils with laughter. Even the Elf laughed at me.

I worked for several weeks. I came in drunk each night. It didn't matter; I had the job nobody wanted. After an hour at the oven I was sober. My hands were blistered and burned. Each day I sat aching in my room pricking my blisters with pins I first sterilized with matches.

ONE NIGHT I was drunker than usual. I refused to punch in. "This is it," I told them.

The Elf was in trauma. "How will we make it, Chinaski?"

"Ah."

"*Give us one more night!*"

I got his head in the crook of my arm, squeezed; his ears turned pink. "Little bastard," I said. Then I let him go.

22

AFTER ARRIVING IN Philadelphia I found a roominghouse and paid a week's rent in advance. The nearest bar was fifty years old. You could smell the odor of urine, shit and vomit of a half century as it came up through the floor into the bar from the restrooms below.

It was 4:30 in the afternoon. Two men were fighting in the center of the bar.

The guy to the right of me said his name was Danny. To the left, he said his name was Jim.

Danny had a cigarette in his mouth, end glowing. An empty beerbottle looped through the air. It missed his cigarette and nose, fractionally. He didn't move or look around, tapped the ashes of his cigarette into a tray. "That was pretty close, you son of a bitch! Come that close again, you got a fight on your hands!"

Every seat was taken. There were women in there, a few housewives, fat and a bit stupid, and two or three ladies who had fallen on hard times. As I sat there one girl got up and left with a man. She was back in five minutes.

"Helen! Helen! How do you do it?"

She laughed.

Another jumped up to try her. "That must be good. I gotta have some!"

They left together. Helen was back in five minutes.

"She must have a suction pump for a pussy!"

"I gotta try me some of that," said an old guy down at the end of the bar. "I haven't had a hard-on since Teddy Roosevelt took his last hill."

It took Helen ten minutes with that one.

"I WANT a sandwich," said a fat guy. "Who's gonna run me an errand for a sandwich?"

I told him I would. "Roast beef on a bun, everything on."

He gave me some money. "Keep the change."

I walked down to the sandwich place. An old geezer with a big belly walked up. "Roast beef on a bun to go, everything on. And a bottle of beer while I'm waiting."

I drank the beer, took the sandwich back to the fat guy in the bar, and found another seat. A shot of whiskey appeared. I drank it down. Another appeared. I drank it down. The juke box played.

A young fellow of about twenty-four came down from the end of the bar. "I need the venetian blinds cleaned," he said to me.

"You sure do."

"What do you do?"

"Nothing. Drink. Both."

"How about the blinds?"

"Five bucks."

"You're hired."

They called him Billy-Boy. Billy-Boy had married the owner of the bar. She was forty-five.

He brought me two buckets, some suds, rags and

sponges. I took the blinds down, removed the slats, and began.

"Drinks are free," said Tommy the night bartender, "as long as you're working."

"Shot of whiskey, Tommy."

IT WAS slow work; the dust had caked, turned into embedded grime. I cut my hands several times on the edges of the metal slats. The soapy water burned.

"Shot of whiskey, Tommy."

I finished one set of blinds and hung them up. The patrons of the bar turned to look at my work.

"Beautiful!"

"It sure helps the place."

"They'll probably raise the price of drinks."

"Shot of whiskey, Tommy," I said.

I took down another set of blinds, pulled out the slats. I beat Jim at the pinball machine for a quarter, then emptied the buckets in the crapper and got fresh water.

The second set went slower. My hands collected more cuts. I doubt that those blinds had been cleaned in ten years. I won another quarter at the pinball then Billy-Boy hollered at me to go back to work.

Helen walked by on her way to the women's crapper.

"Helen, I'll give you five bucks when I'm finished. Will that cover?"

"Sure, but you won't be able to get it up after all that work."

"I'll get it up."

"I'll be here at closing. If you can still stand up, then you can have it for nothing!"

"I'll be standing *tall*, baby."

Helen walked back to the crapper.

"Shot of whiskey, Tommy."

"Hey, take it easy," said Billy-Boy, "or you'll never finish that job tonight."

"Billy, if I don't finish you keep your five."

"It's a deal. All you people hear that?"

"We heard you, Billy, you cheap ass."

"One for the road, Tommy."

Tommy gave me the whiskey. I drank it and went to work. I drove myself on. After a number of whiskeys I had the three sets of blinds up and shining.

"All right, Billy, pay up."

"You're not finished."

"What?"

"There's three more windows in the back room."

"The back room?"

"The back room. The party room."

Billy-Boy showed me the back room. There were three more windows, three more sets of blinds.

"I'll settle for two-fifty, Billy."

"No, you got to do them all or no pay."

I got my buckets, dumped the water, put in clean water, soap, then took down a set of blinds. I pulled the slats out, put them on a table and stared at them.

Jim stopped on his way to the crapper. "What's the matter?"

"I can't go another slat."

When Jim came out of the crapper he went to the bar and brought back his beer. He began cleaning the blinds.

"Jim, forget it."

I went to the bar, got another whiskey. When I got back one of the girls was taking down a set of blinds. "Be careful, don't cut yourself," I told her.

A few minutes later there were four or five people back there talking and laughing, even Helen. They were all working on the blinds. Soon nearly everybody in the bar was back there. I worked in two more whiskeys. Finally the blinds were finished and hanging. It hadn't taken very long. They sparkled. Billy-Boy came in:

"I don't have to pay you."

"The job's finished."

"But you didn't finish it."

"Don't be a cheap shit, Billy," somebody said.

Billy-Boy dug out the $5 and I took it. We moved to the bar. "A drink for everybody!" I laid the $5 down. "And one for me too."

Tommy went around pouring drinks.

I drank my drink and Tommy picked up the $5.

"You owe the bar $3.15."

"Put it on the tab."

"O.K., what's your last name?"

"Chinaski."

"You heard the one about the Polack who went to the outhouse?"

"Yes."

Drinks came my way until closing time. After the last one I looked around. Helen had slipped out. Helen had lied.

Just like a bitch, I thought, afraid of the long hard ride . . .

I got up and walked back to my roominghouse. The moonlight was bright. My footsteps echoed in the empty street and it sounded as if somebody was following me. I looked around. I was mistaken. I was quite alone.

23

WHEN I ARRIVED in St. Louis it was very cold, about to snow, and I found a room in a nice clean place, a room on the second floor, in the back. It was early evening and I was having one of my depressive fits so I went to bed early and somehow managed to sleep.

When I awakened in the morning it was very cold. I was shivering uncontrollably. I got up and found that one of the windows was open. I closed the window and went back to bed. I began to feel nauseated. I managed to sleep another hour, then awakened. I got up, dressed, barely made it to the hall bathroom and vomited. I undressed and got back into bed. Soon there was a knock on the door. I didn't answer. The knocking continued. "Yes?" I asked.

"Are you all right?"

"Yes."

"Can we come in?"

"Come in."

There were two girls. One was a bit on the fat side but scrubbed, shining, in a flowery pink dress. She had a kind face. The other wore a wide tight belt that accentuated her very good figure. Her hair was long, dark, and she had a cute nose; she wore high heels, had perfect legs, and wore a white low cut blouse. Her eyes were dark brown, very dark, and they kept looking at me, amused, very amused. "I'm Gertrude," she said, "and this is Hilda."

Hilda managed to blush as Gertrude moved across the room toward my bed. "We heard you in the bathroom. Are you sick?"

"Yes. But it's nothing serious, I'm sure. An open window."

"Mrs. Downing, the landlady, is making you some soup."

"No, it's all right."

"It'll do you good."

Gertrude moved nearer my bed. Hilda remained where she was, pink and scrubbed and blushing. Gertrude pivoted back and forth on her very high heels. "Are you new in town?"

"Yes."

"You're not in the army?"

"No."

"What do you do?"

"Nothing."

"No work?"

"No work."

"Yes," said Gertrude to Hilda, "look at his hands. He has the most beautiful hands. You can see that he has never worked."

The landlady, Mrs. Downing, knocked. She was large and pleasant. I imagined that her husband was dead and that she was religious. She carried a large bowl of beef broth, holding it high in the air. I could see the steam rising. I took the bowl. We exchanged pleasantries. Yes, her husband was dead. She was very religious. There were crackers, plus salt and pepper.

"Thank you."

Mrs. Downing looked at both of the girls. "We'll all be going now. We hope you get well soon. And I hope the girls haven't bothered you too much?"

"Oh no!" I grinned into the broth. She liked that.

"Come on, girls."

Mrs. Downing left the door open. Hilda managed one last blush, gave me the tiniest smile, then left. Gertrude remained. She watched me spoon the broth in. "Is it good?"

"I want to thank all you people. All this . . . is very unusual."

"I'm going." She turned and walked very slowly toward the door. Her buttocks moved under her tight black skirt; her legs were golden. At the doorway she stopped and turned, rested her dark eyes on me once again, held me. I was transfixed, glowing. The moment she felt my response she tossed her head and laughed. She had a lovely neck, and all that dark hair. She walked off down the hall, leaving the door ajar.

I took the salt and pepper, seasoned the broth, broke the crackers into it, and spooned it into my illness.

24

I FOUND A job as a shipping clerk in a ladies' dresswear shop. Even during World War II when there was supposed to be a manpower shortage there were four or five applicants for each job. (At least for the menial jobs.) We waited with our application forms filled out. Born? Single? Married? Draft status? Last job? Last jobs? Why did you leave? I had filled out so many job forms that long ago I had memorized the right answers. Having gotten out of bed quite late that morning I was the last to be called. A bald man with strange tufts of hair over each ear interviewed me.

"Yes?" he asked, looking at me over the sheet.

"I'm a writer temporarily down on my inspirations."

"Oh, a *writer*, eh?"

"Yes."

"Are you sure?"

"No, I'm not."

"What do you write?"

"Short stories mostly. And I'm halfway through a novel."

"A novel, eh?"

"Yes."

"What's the name of it?"

" 'The Leaky Faucet of My Doom.' "

"Oh, I like that. What's it about?"

"Everything."

"Everything? You mean, for instance, it's about cancer?"

"Yes."

"How about my wife?"

"She's in there too."

You don't say. Why do you want to work in a ladies' dress shop?"

"I've always liked ladies in ladies' dresses."

"Are you 4-F?"

"Yes."

"Let me see your draft card."

I showed him my draft card. He handed it back.

"You're hired."

25

WE WERE DOWN in a cellar. The walls were painted yellow. We packed our ladies' dresses into oblong cardboard boxes about three feet long and a foot or a foot and a half wide. A certain skill was needed in folding each dress so that it did not become creased in the carton. To prevent this we used cardboard fillers and tissue, and were given careful instructions. The U.S. Mail was used for out of town deliveries. We each had our own scale and our own postage meter machine. No smoking.

Larabee was the head shipping clerk. Klein was the assistant head shipping clerk. Larabee was the boss. Klein was trying to move Larabee out of his job. Klein was Jewish and the owners of the store were Jewish and Larabee was nervous. Klein and Larabee argued and fought all day long and on into the evenings. Yes, evenings. The problem, as it was in those days during the war, was overtime. Those in control always preferred to overwork a few men continually, instead of hiring more people so everyone might work less. You gave the boss eight hours, and he always asked for more. He never sent you home after six hours, for example. You might have time to think.

26

WHENEVER I WENT out into the hall of the roominghouse Gertrude seemed to be standing there. She was perfect, pure maddening sex, and she knew it, and she played on it, dripped it, and allowed you to suffer for it. It made her happy. I didn't feel too bad either. She could easily have shut me out and not even have allowed me to be warmed by a glimpse of it. Like most men in that situation I realized that I wouldn't get anything out of her—intimate talks, exciting roller-coaster rides, long Sunday afternoon walks—until after I had made some odd promises.

"You're a strange guy. You stay alone a lot, don't you?"

"Yes."

"What's wrong?"

"I was sick long before that morning you met me."

"Are you sick now?"

"No."

"Then what's wrong?"

"I don't like people."

"Do you think that's right?"

"Probably not."

"Will you take me to a movie some night?"

"I'll try."

Gertrude swayed in front of me; she swayed on her high heels. She moved forward. Bits of her were touching me. I simply couldn't respond. There was a space between us. The distance was too great. I felt as if she was talking to a person who had vanished, a person who was no longer there, no longer alive. Her eyes seemed to look right through me. I couldn't make a connection with her. I didn't feel shame for that, only rather embarrassed, and helpless.

"Come with me."

"What?"

"I want to show you my bedroom."

I followed Gertrude down the hall. She opened her bedroom door and I followed her in. It was a very feminine room. The large bed was covered with stuffed animals. All of the animals looked surprised and stared at me: giraffes, bears, lions, dogs. The air was perfumed. Everything was neat and clean and looked soft and comfortable. Gertrude moved close to me.

"You like my bedroom?"

"It's nice. Oh yes, I like it."

"Don't ever tell Mrs. Downing that I asked you in here, she'd be scandalized."

"I won't tell."

Gertrude stood there, silently.

"I have to go," I told her finally. Then I went to the door, opened it, closed it behind me, and walked back to my room.

27

AFTER LOSING SEVERAL typewriters to pawnbrokers I simply gave up the idea of owning one. I printed out my stories by hand and sent them out that way. I hand-printed them with a pen. I got to be a very fast hand-printer. It got so that I could hand-print faster than I could write. I wrote three or four short stories a week. I kept things in the mail. I imagined the editors of *The Atlantic Monthly* and *Harper's* saying: "Hey, here's another one of those things by that nut . . ."

One night I took Gertrude to a bar. We sat at a table to one side and drank beer. It was snowing outside. I felt a little better than usual. We drank and talked. An hour or so passed. I began gazing into Gertrude's eyes and she looked right back. "*A good man, nowadays, is hard to find!*"

said the juke box. Gertrude moved her body to the music, moved her head to the music, and looked into my eyes.

"You have a very strange face," she said. "You're not really ugly."

"Number four shipping clerk, working his way up."

"Have you ever been in love?"

"Love is for real people."

"You sound real."

"I dislike real people."

"You dislike them?"

"I hate them."

We drank some more, not saying much. It continued to snow. Gertrude turned her head and stared into the crowd of people. Then she looked at me.

"Isn't he *handsome?*"

"Who?"

"That soldier over there. He's sitting alone. He sits so *straight*. And he's got all his medals on."

"Come on, let's get out of here."

"But it's not late."

"You can stay."

"No, I want to go with *you*."

"I don't care what you do."

"Is it the soldier? Are you mad because of the soldier?"

"Oh, shit!"

"It was the soldier!"

"I'm going."

I stood up at the table, left a tip and walked toward the door. I heard Gertrude behind me. I walked down the street in the snow. Soon she was walking at my side.

"You didn't even get a taxi. These high heels in the snow!"

I didn't answer. We walked the four or five blocks to the rooming house. I went up the steps with her beside me. Then I walked down to my room, opened the door, closed it, got out of my clothes and went to bed. I heard her throw something against the wall of her room.

28

I KEPT HAND-PRINTING my short stories. I sent most of them to Clay Gladmore, whose New York mag *Frontfire* I admired. They only paid $25 a story but Gladmore had discovered William Saroyan and many others, had been Sherwood Anderson's buddy. Gladmore returned many of my things with personal rejections. True, most of them weren't very long but they did seem kind and they were encouraging. The larger magazines used printed rejection slips. Even Gladmore's printed slips seemed to have some warmth to them: "We regret, alas, that this is a rejection slip but . . ."

So I kept Gladmore busy with four or five stories a week. Meanwhile I was in ladies's dresswear, down in the cellar. Klein still hadn't ousted Larabee; Cox, the other shipping clerk, didn't care who was ousted as long as he could sneak his smoke on the stairway every twenty-five minutes.

Overtime became automatic. I drank more and more in my off hours. The eight hour day was gone forever. In the morning when you walked in you might as well settle for at least eleven hours. This included Saturdays, which used to be half-days, but which had turned into full days. The war was on but the ladies were buying the hell out of dresses . . .

It was after one twelve hour day. I had gotten into my coat, had come up out of the cellar, had lighted a cigarette and was walking along the hallway toward the exit when I heard the boss's voice: "Chinaski!"

"Yes?"

"Step in here."

My boss was smoking a long expensive cigar. He looked well-rested.

"This is my friend, Carson Gentry."

Carson Gentry was also smoking a long expensive cigar.

"Mr. Gentry is a writer too. He is very interested in writing. I told him that you were a writer and he wanted to meet you. You don't mind, do you?"

"No I don't mind."

They both sat there looking at me and smoking their cigars. Several minutes passed. They inhaled, exhaled, looked at me.

"Do you mind if I leave?" I asked.

"It's all right," said my boss.

29

I ALWAYS WALKED to my room, it was six or seven blocks away. The trees along the streets were all alike: small, twisted, half-frozen, leafless. I liked them. I walked along under the cold moon.

That scene in the office stayed with me. Those cigars, the fine clothes. I thought of good steaks, long rides up winding driveways that led to beautiful homes. Ease. Trips to Europe. Fine women. Were they that much more clever than I? The only difference was money, and the desire to accumulate it.

I'd do it too! I'd save my pennies. I'd get an idea, I'd spring a loan. I'd hire and fire. I'd keep whiskey in my desk drawer. I'd have a wife with size 40 breasts and an ass that would make the paperboy on the corner come in his pants when he saw it wobble. I'd cheat on her and she'd know it and keep silent in order to live in my house with my wealth. I'd fire men just to see the look of dismay on their faces. I'd fire women who didn't deserve to be fired.

That was all a man needed: hope. It was lack of hope that discouraged a man. I remembered my New Orleans days, living on two five-cent candy bars a day for weeks at a time in order to have leisure to write. But starvation, unfortunately, didn't improve art. It only hindered it. A man's soul was rooted in his stomach. A man could write much better after eating a porterhouse steak and drinking a pint of whiskey than he could ever write after eating a nickel candy bar. The myth of the starving artist was a hoax. Once you realized that everything was a hoax you got wise and began to bleed and burn your fellow man. I'd build an empire upon the broken bodies and lives of helpless men, women, and children—I'd shove it to them all the way. *I'd show them!*

I was at my rooming house. I walked up the stairway to the door of my room. I unlocked the door, turned on the light. Mrs. Downing had put the mail by my door. There was a large brown envelope from Gladmore. I picked it up. It was heavy with rejected manuscripts. I sat down and opened the envelope.

Dear Mr. Chinaski:

We are returning these four stories but we are keeping *My Beerdrunk Soul is Sadder Than All The Dead Christmas Trees Of The World.* We have been watching your work for a long time and we are most happy to accept this story.

Sincerely,
Clay Gladmore.

I got up from the chair still holding my acceptance slip. MY FIRST. From the number one literary magazine in America. Never had the world looked so good, so full of promise. I walked over to the bed, sat down, read it again. I studied each curve in the handwriting of Gladmore's signature. I got up, walked the acceptance slip over to the dresser, propped it there. Then I undressed, turned out the lights and went to bed. I couldn't sleep. I got up, turned on the light, walked over to the dresser and read it again:

Dear Mr. Chinaski . . .

30

I OFTEN SAW Gertrude in the hall. We talked but I didn't ask her out again. She stood very close to me, gently swaying, now and then staggering, as if drunk, upon her very high heels. One Sunday morning I found myself on the front lawn with Gertrude and Hilda. The girls made snowballs, laughed and screamed, threw them at me. Never having lived in snow country I was slow at first but I soon found out how to make a snowball and hurl it. Gertrude fired up, screamed. She was delicious. She was all flare and lightning. For a moment I felt like walking across the lawn and grabbing her. Then I gave up, walked away down the street with the snowballs whizzing past me.

Tens of thousands of young men were fighting in Europe and China, in the Pacific Islands. When they came back she'd find one. She wouldn't have any problem. Not with that body. Not with those eyes. Even Hilda wouldn't have any difficulty.

I BEGAN to feel that it was time for me to leave St. Louis. I decided to go back to Los Angeles; meanwhile I kept handprinting short stories by the score, got drunk, listened to Beethoven's Fifth, Brahms' Second . . .

ONE PARTICULAR night after work I stopped at a local bar. I sat and drank five or six beers, got up and walked the block or so to my roominghouse. Gertrude's door was open as I walked past. "Henry . . ."

"Hello." I walked up to the door, looked at her. "Gertrude, I'm leaving town. I gave notice at work today."

"Oh, I'm sorry."

"You people have been nice to me."

"Listen, before you leave I want you to meet my boyfriend."

"Your boyfriend?"

"Yes, he just moved in, right down the hall."

I followed her. She knocked and I stood behind her. The door opened: grey and white striped pants; long-sleeved checked shirt; necktie. A thin moustache. Vacant eyes. Out of one of his nostrils streamed a nearly invisible thread of snot that had finally gathered into a little gleaming ball. The ball had settled in the moustache and was gathering to drip off, but meanwhile it sat there and reflected the light.

"Joey," she said, "I want you to meet Henry."

We shook hands. Gertrude went in. The door closed. I walked back to my room and began packing. Packing was always a good time.

31

WHEN I GOT back to Los Angeles I found a cheap hotel just off Hoover Street and stayed in bed and drank. I drank for some time, three or four days. I couldn't get myself to read the want ads. The thought of sitting in front of a man behind a desk and telling him that I wanted a job, that I was qualified for a job, was too much for me. Frankly, I was horrified by life, at what a man had to do simply in order to eat, sleep, and keep himself clothed. So I stayed in bed and drank. When you drank the world was still out there, but for the moment it didn't have you by the throat.

I got out of bed one night, dressed and walked up town. I found myself on Alvarado Street. I walked along until I came to an inviting bar and went in. It was crowded. There was only one seat left at the bar. I sat in it. I ordered a scotch and water. To my right sat a rather dark blonde, gone a bit to fat, neck and cheeks now flabby, obviously a drunk; but there was a certain lingering beauty to her features, and her body still looked firm and young and well-shaped. In fact, her legs were long and lovely. When the lady finished her drink I asked her if she wanted another. She said yes. I bought her one.

"Buncha damn fools in here," she said.

"Everywhere, but especially in here," I said.

I paid for three or four more rounds. We didn't speak. Then I told the lady, "That drink was it. I'm broke."

"Are you serious?"

"Yes."

"Do you have a place to stay?"

"An apartment, two or three days left on the rent."

"And you don't have any money? Or anything to drink?"

"No."

"Come with me."

I followed her out of the bar. I noticed that she had a very nice behind. I walked with her to the nearest liquor store. She told the clerk what she wanted: two fifths of Grandad, a sixpack of beer, two packs of cigarettes, some chips, some mixed nuts, some alka-seltzer, a good cigar. The clerk tabbed it up. "Charge it," she said, "to Wilbur Oxnard." "Wait," he said, "I'll have to phone." The clerk dialed a number and spoke over the phone. Then he hung up. "It's all right," he said. I helped her with her bags and we walked out.

"Where are we going with this stuff?"

"To your place. Do you have a car?"

I took her to my car. I had bought one off a lot in
Compton for thirty-five dollars. It had broken springs and
a leaking radiator, but it ran.

We got to my place and I put the stuff in the
refrigerator, poured two drinks, brought them out, sat
down and lit my cigar. She sat on the couch across from
me, her legs crossed. She had on green earrings. "Swell,"
she said.

"What?"

"You think you're Swell, you think you're Hot Shit!"

"No."

"Yes, you do. I can tell by the way you act. I still like
you. I liked you right off."

"Pull your dress a little higher."

"You like legs?"

"Yeh. Pull your dress a little higher."

She did. "Oh, Jesus, now higher, higher yet!"

"Listen, you're not some kind of nut, are you? There's
one guy been bothering the girls, he picks them up, then
takes them to his place, strips them down and cuts
crossword puzzles into their bodies with a pen knife."

"I'm not him."

"Then there are guys who fuck you and then chop you
up into little pieces. They find part of your asshole stuffed
up a drainpipe in Playa Del Rey and your left tit in a
trashcan down at Oceanside . . ."

"I stopped doing that years ago. Lift your skirt higher."

She hiked her skirt higher. It was like the beginning of
life and laughter, it was the real meaning of the sun. I
walked over, sat on the couch next to her and kissed her.
Then I got up, poured two more drinks and tuned the
radio in to KFAC. We caught the beginning of something
by Debussy.

"You like that kind of music?" she asked.

* * *

SOME TIME during the night as we were talking I fell off the couch. I lay on the floor and looked up those beautiful legs. "Baby," I said, "I'm a genius but nobody knows it but me."

She looked down at me. "Get up off the floor you damn fool and get me a drink."

I brought her drink and curled up next to her. I did feel foolish. Later we got into bed. The lights were off and I got on top of her. I stroked once or twice, stopped. "What's your name, anyhow?"

"What the hell difference does it make?" she answered.

32

HER NAME WAS Laura. It was 2 o'clock in the afternoon and I walked along the path behind the furniture shop on Alvarado Street. I had my suitcase with me. There was a large white house back there, wooden, two stories, old, the white paint peeling. "Now stay back from the door," she said. "There's a mirror halfway up the stairs that allows him to see who's at the door."

Laura stood there ringing the bell while I hid to the right of the door. "Let him just see me, and when the buzzer sounds, I'll push the door open and you follow me in."

The buzzer rang and Laura pushed the door open. I followed her in, leaving my suitcase at the bottom of the stairs. Wilbur Oxnard stood at the top of the stairway and Laura ran up to him. Wilbur was an old guy, grey-haired, with one arm. "Baby, so *good* to see you!" Wilbur put his one arm around Laura and kissed her. When they separated he saw me.

"Who's that guy?"

"Oh, Willie, I want you to meet a friend of mine."

"Hi," I said.

Wilbur didn't answer me. "Wilbur Oxnard, Henry Chinaski," Laura introduced us.

"Good to know you, Wilbur," I said.

Wilbur still didn't answer. Finally he said, "Well, come on up."

I followed Wilbur and Laura across the front room. There were coins all over the floor, nickels, dimes, quarters, halves. An electric organ sat in the very center of the room. I followed them into the kitchen where we sat down at the breakfastnook table. Laura introduced me to the two women who sat there. "Henry, this is Grace and this is Jerry. Girls, this is Henry Chinaski."

"Hello, there," said Grace.

"How are you doing?" asked Jerry.

"My pleasure, ladies."

They were drinking whiskey with beer chasers. A bowl was in the center of the table filled with black and green olives, chili peppers, and celery hearts. I reached out and got a chili pepper. "Help yourself," Wilbur said, waving toward the whiskey bottle. He'd already put a beer down in front of me. I poured a drink.

"What do you do?" asked Wilbur.

"He's a writer," said Laura. "He's been printed in the magazines."

"Are you a writer?" Wilbur asked me.

"Sometimes."

"I need a writer. Are you a good one?"

"Every writer thinks he's a good one."

"I need somebody to do the libretto for an opera I've written. It's called 'The Emperor of San Francisco.' Did you know there was once a guy who wanted to be the Emperor of San Francisco?"

"No, no, I didn't."

"It's very interesting. I'll give you a book on it."

"All right."

We sat quietly a while, drinking. All the girls were in their mid-thirties, attractive and very sexy, and they knew it.

"How do you like the curtains?" he asked me. "The girls made these curtains for me. The girls have a lot of talent."

I looked at the curtains. They were sickening. Huge red strawberries all over them, surrounded by dripping stems.

"I like the curtains," I told him.

Wilbur got out some more beer and we all had more drinks from the whiskey bottle. "Don't worry," said Wilbur, "there's another bottle when this one's gone."

"Thanks, Wilbur."

He looked at me. "My arm's getting stiff." He lifted his arm and moved his fingers. "I can hardly move my fingers, I think I'm going to die. The doctors can't figure out what's wrong. The girls think I'm kidding, the girls laugh at me."

"I don't think you're kidding," I told him, "I believe you."

We had a couple of drinks more.

"I like you," said Wilbur, "you look like you've been around, you look like you've got class. Most people don't have class. You've got class."

"I don't know anything about class," I said, "but I've been around."

"Let's go into the other room. I want to play you a few choruses from the opera."

"Fine," I said.

We opened a new fifth, got out some more beer, and went into the other room. "Don't you want me to make you some soup, Wilbur?" asked Grace.

"Who ever heard of eating soup at the organ?" he answered.

We all laughed. We all liked Wilbur.

"He throws money on the floor every time he gets drunk," Laura whispered to me. "He says nasty things to us and throws coins at us. He says it's what we're worth. He can get very nasty."

Wilbur got up, went to his bedroom, came out wearing a sailing cap, and sat back down at the organ. He began playing the organ with his one arm and his bad fingers. He played a very loud organ. We sat there drinking and listening to the organ. When he finished, I applauded.

Wilbur turned around on the stool. "The girls were up here the other night," he said, "and then somebody hollered 'RAID!' You should have seen them running, some of them naked, some of them in panties and bras, they all ran out and hid in the garage. It was funny as hell. I sat up here and they came drifting back, one by one, from the garage. It was sure *funny!*"

"Who hollered 'RAID'?" I asked.

"I did," he said.

Then he stood up and walked into his bedroom and began undressing. I could see him sitting on the edge of his bed in his underwear. Laura walked in and sat on the bed with him and kissed him. Then she came out and Grace and Jerry went in. Laura motioned to the bottom of the stairway. I went down for my suitcase and brought it back up.

33

WHEN WE AWAKENED, Laura told me about Wilbur. It was 9:30 a.m. and there wasn't a sound in the house. "He's a millionaire," she said, "don't let this old house fool you. His grandfather bought land all around here and his father did too. Grace is his girl but Grace gives him a rough time.

And he's a tight son of a bitch. He likes to take care of the girls in the bars who have no place to sleep. But all he gives them is food and a bed, never any money. And they only get drinks when *he's* drinking. Jerry got to him one night, though. He was horny and chasing her around the table and she said, 'No, no no, not unless you give me fifty bucks a month for life!' He finally signed a piece of paper and do you know it held up in court? He has to pay her fifty bucks a month, and it's fixed so that when he dies his family will have to pay her."

"Good," I said.

"Grace is his main girl, though."

"How about you?"

"Not for a long time."

"That's good, because I like you."

"You do?"

"Yes."

"Now, you watch. If he comes out this morning with his sailor cap on, that captain's cap, that means we're going out on the yacht. The doctor told him to get a yacht for his health."

"Is it a big one?"

"Sure. Listen, did you pick up all those coins off the floor last night?"

"Yes," I said.

"It's better to take some and leave some."

"I guess you're right. Should I put some back?"

"If you get a chance."

I started to get up to get dressed when Jerry ran into the bedroom. "He's standing in front of the mirror adjusting his cap to the proper angle. We're going out on the yacht!"

"O.K., Jerry," said Laura.

We both began to get dressed. We were just in time. Wilbur didn't speak. He was hungover. We followed him down the stairway and into the garage where we got into an unbelievably old car. It was so old it had a rumble seat. Grace and Jerry got into the front seat with Wilbur and I got into the rumble seat with Laura. Wilbur backed out the driveway, headed south on Alvarado, and we were on our way to San Pedro.

"He's hungover and he's not drinking and when he's not drinking he doesn't want anybody else to drink either, the bastard. So watch it," said Laura.

"Hell, I need a drink."

"We all need a drink," she said. Laura took a pint from her purse and unscrewed the cap. She handed the bottle to me. "Now wait until he checks us in the rear-view mirror. Then the minute his eyes go back to the road, take a slug."

Soon I saw Wilbur's eyes looking at us in the rear-view mirror. Then he looked back at the road. I took a hit and felt much better. I handed the bottle back to Laura. She waited until Wilbur's eyes looked into the rear-view, then went back to the road. She had her turn. It was a pleasant journey. By the time we reached San Pedro the bottle was empty. Laura took out some gum, I lit a cigar, and we climbed out. As I helped Laura out of the rumble seat her skirt came up and I saw those long nylon legs, the knees, the slender ankles. I began to get horny and looked out over the water. There was the yacht: *The Oxwill*. It was the largest yacht in the harbor. A small motor boat took us out. We climbed aboard. Wilbur waved to some fellow boatmen and some wharf-rats and then he looked at me.

"How you feeling?"

"Great, Wilbur, great . . . like an Emperor."

"Come here, I want to show you something." We walked toward the back of the boat and Wilbur leaned down and pulled a ring. He pulled back a hatch cover. There were two motors down there. "I want to show you how to start this auxiliary motor in case anything goes wrong. It's not difficult. I can do it with one arm."

I stood there bored as Wilbur pulled at a rope. I nodded and told him that I understood. But that wasn't enough, he had to show me how to pull anchor and unmoor from the dock when all I wanted was another drink.

After all that, we pulled out and he stood there in the cabin with his sailor's cap on, steering the yacht. All the girls crowded around him.

"Oh, Willie, let me steer!"

"Willie, let *me* steer!"

I didn't ask to steer. I didn't want to steer. I followed Laura down below. It was like a luxury hotel suite, only there were bunks on the wall, no beds. We went to the refrigerator. It was filled with food and drink. We found an open fifth of whiskey and took that out. We had a bit of whiskey and water. It seemed like a decent life. Laura turned on the record player and we listened to something called "Bonaparte's Retreat." Laura looked fine. She was happy and smiling. I leaned over and kissed her, ran my hand up her leg. Then I heard the engine cut off and Wilbur came down the steps.

"We're going back in," he said. He looked quite stern in his captain's cap.

"What for?" asked Laura.

"She's gone into one of her moods. I'm afraid she'll jump overboard. She won't speak to me. She just sits there, staring. She can't swim. I'm afraid she'll jump into the ocean."

"Listen, Wilbur," said Laura, "just give her ten bucks. She's got runs in her stockings."

"No, we're going in. Besides, you people have been *drinking!*"

Wilbur went back up the steps. The engine coughed and we turned around and headed back toward San Pedro.

"This happens everytime we try to go to Catalina. Grace goes into one of her moods and sits there staring at the ocean with that scarf tied around her head. That's how she gets things out of him. She's never going to jump overboard. She hates water."

"Well," I said, "we might as well have a few more drinks. When I think about writing lyrics to Wilbur's opera I realize how disgusting my life has become."

"We might as well drink up," said Laura, "he's mad now anyhow."

Jerry came down and joined us. "Grace is sore about that fifty bucks a month I'm getting out of his ass. Hell, it ain't that easy. The minute she's gone that old son of a bitch leaps on top of me and starts pumping. He never gets enough. He's afraid he's going to die and he wants to get in as many as possible."

She drank her shot and poured another one.

"I should have stayed in personnel at Sears Roebuck. I had a good thing going."

We all drank to that.

34

By THE TIME we docked, Grace had joined us too. She still had the scarf around her head and she wasn't talking but she was drinking. We were all drinking. We were all drinking when Wilbur came down the stairs. He stood there looking at us. "I'll be right back," he said.

That was in the afternoon. We waited and we drank. The girls started arguing about how they should handle Wilbur. I climbed into one of the bunks and went to sleep. When I awakened it was evening going into night and it was cold.

"Where's Wilbur?" I asked.

"He's not coming back," said Jerry, "he's mad."

"He'll be back," said Laura, "Grace is here."

"I don't give a damn if he never comes back," said Grace. "We got enough food and drink here to supply the whole Egyptian Army for a month."

So there I was in the biggest yacht in the harbor with three women. But it was very cold. It was the chill off the water. I got out of the bunk, got a drink, and crawled back into the bunk. "Jesus, it's cold," said Jerry, "let me get in there and warm up." She kicked off her shoes and climbed into the bunk with me. Laura and Grace were drunk and arguing about something. Jerry was small and round, very round, a snug type. She pushed against me.

"Jesus, it's cold. Put your arms around me."

"Laura . . ." I said.

"Fuck Laura."

"I mean, she might get mad."

"She won't get mad. We're friends. Look." Jerry sat up in the bunk. "Laura, Laura . . ."

"Yes?"

"Look, I'm trying to get warm. O.K.?"

"O.K.," said Laura.

Jerry snuggled back down under the covers. "See, she said it's O.K."

"All right," I said. I put my hand on her ass and kissed her.

"Just don't go too far," said Laura.

"He's just holding me," said Jerry.

I got my hand up under her dress and began working her panties down. It was difficult. By the time she kicked them off I was more than ready. Her tongue shot in and out of my mouth. We tried to look nonchalant while we did it sideways. I slipped out several times but Jerry put it back in. "Don't go too far," Laura said again. It slipped out and Jerry grabbed it and squeezed. "She's just holding me," I told Laura. Jerry giggled and put it back in. It stayed there. I got hotter and hotter. "You bitch," I whispered, "I love

57

you." Then I came. Jerry got out of the bunk and went to the bathroom. Grace was making us roast beef sandwiches. I climbed out of the bunk and we had roast beef sandwiches, potato salad, sliced tomatoes, coffee and apple pie. We were all hungry.

"I sure got warmed up," said Jerry. "Henry's one good heating pad."

"I'm plenty cold," said Grace, "I think I'll try some of that heating pad. Do you mind, Laura?"

"I don't mind. Just don't go too far."

"How far's too far?"

"You know what I mean."

After we ate I got into the bunk and Grace climbed in with me. She was the tallest of the three. I'd never been in bed with a woman that tall. I kissed her. Her tongue answered. Women, I thought, women are magic. What marvelous beings they are! I reached up under her dress and pulled at the panties. It was a long way down. "What the hell are you doing?" she whispered. "I'm pulling your panties down." "What for?" "I'm going to fuck you." "I just want to get warm." "I'm going to fuck you." "Laura is my friend. I'm Wilbur's woman." "I'm going to fuck you." "What are you doing?" "I'm trying to get it in." "No!" "God damn it, help me." "Get it in yourself." "Help me." "Get it in by yourself. Laura's my friend." "What's that got to do with it?" "What?" "Forget it." "Listen, I'm not ready yet." "Here's my finger." "Ow, easy. Show a lady some respect." "All right, all right. Is that better?" "That's better. Higher. There. There! That's it . . ."

"No hanky-panky now," said Laura.

"No, I'm just warming her up."

"I wonder when Wilbur's coming back?" said Jerry.

"I don't give a damn if he never comes back," I said, getting it into Grace. She moaned. It was good. I went very slow, measuring my strokes. I didn't slip out like with

Jerry. "You rotten son of a bitch," said Grace, "you bastard, Laura's my friend." "I'm fucking you," I said, "feel that thing going in and out of your body, in and out, in and out, in and out, flup flup flup." "Don't talk like that, you're making me hot." "I'm fucking you," I said, "fuck fuck fucky fuck, we're fucking, we're fucking, we're fucking. Oh, it's so *dirty*, oh it's so filthy, this fucking fucking fucking ..." "God damn you, stop it." "It's getting bigger and bigger, feel it?" "Yes, yes ..." "I'm going to come. Jesus Christ, I'm going to come ..." I came and pulled out. "You raped me, you bastard, you raped me," she whispered. "I ought to tell Laura." "Go ahead, tell her. Think she'll believe you?" Grace climbed out of the bunk and went to the bathroom. I wiped off on the sheet, pulled up my pants and leaped out of the bunk.

"You girls know how to play dice?"

"What do you need?" asked Laura.

"I've got the dice. You girls got any money? It takes dice and money. I'll show you how. Get your money out and put it in front of you. Don't be embarrassed if you don't have much money. I don't have much money. We're all friends, aren't we?"

"Yes," said Jerry, "we're all friends."

"Yes," said Laura, "we're all friends."

Grace came out of the bathroom. "What's that bastard doing now?"

"He's going to show us how to play dice," said Jerry.

"*Shoot dice* is the term. I'm going to show you girls how to *shoot dice*."

"You are, eh?" asked Grace.

"Yeah, Grace, get your tall ass down here and I'll show you how it works ..."

An hour later I had most of the money when Wilbur Oxnard suddenly came down the steps. That's how Willie found us when he came back—shooting craps and drunk.

"*I don't allow gambling on this ship!*" he screamed from the bottom of the steps. Grace got off her knees, walked across the room, put her arms around him and stuck her long tongue into his mouth, then grabbed his private parts. "Where's my Willie been, leavin' his Gracie all alone and lonely on this big boat? I sure missed my Willie."

Willie came into the room smiling. He sat down at the table and Grace got a new fifth of whiskey and opened it. Wilbur poured the drinks. He looked at me:

"I had to go back and straighten out a few notes in the opera. You're still going to do the libretto?"

"The libretto?"

"The words."

"To be truthful, Wilbur, I haven't been thinking much about it, but if you're really serious I'll go to work on it."

"I'm really serious," he said.

"I'll start tomorrow," I said.

Just then Grace reached under the table and unzipped Wilbur's fly. It was going to be a good night for all of us.

35

GRACE, LAURA AND I were sitting at the bar in The Green Smear a few days later when Jerry walked in. "Whiskey sour," she told the barkeep. When the drink came Jerry just stared down at it. "Listen, Grace, you weren't there last night. I was there with Wilbur."

"That's all right, honey, I had a little business to take care of. I like to keep the old boy guessing."

"Grace, he got down low, real low. Henry wasn't there, Laura wasn't there. He had nobody to talk to. I tried to help him."

Laura and I had slept over at an all-night party at the bartender's house. We'd come right from there back to the bar. I hadn't started work on the libretto and Wilbur had been after me. He wanted me to read all the damned books. I'd long ago given up reading anything.

"He was really drinking. He got onto vodka. He started drinking straight vodka. He kept asking where you were Grace."

"That could be love," said Grace.

Jerry finished her whiskey sour and ordered another. "I didn't want him to drink too much," she said, "so when he passed out I took the bottle of vodka, poured out part of it, and filled the rest with water. But he'd already drunk a lot of that hundred proof shit. I kept telling him to come to bed . . ."

"Oh yeah?" said Grace.

"I kept telling him to come to bed but he wouldn't. He was so freaked out that I had to drink too. Anyhow, I got sleepy, it got to me and I left him in that chair with his vodka."

"You didn't get him to bed?" asked Grace.

"No. In the morning I walked in and he was still sitting in that chair, the vodka at his side. 'Good morning, Willie,' I said. I never saw such beautiful eyes. The window was open and the sunlight was in them, all the soul."

"I know," said Grace, "Willie has beautiful eyes."

"He didn't answer me. I couldn't get him to talk. I went to the phone and called his brother, you know, the doctor who takes dope. His brother came up and looked at him and got on the phone and we sat there until two guys came up and they closed Willie's eyes and stuck a needle into him. Then we sat around and talked for a while until one of the guys looked at his watch and said, 'O.K.' and they got up and took Willie off the chair and laid him out on a stretcher. Then they carried him out of there and that was it."

"Shit," said Grace. "I'm fucked."

"You're fucked," said Jerry, "I still got my fifty a month."

"And your round, fat ass," said Grace.

"And my round, fat ass," said Jerry.

Laura and I knew we were fucked. There was no need to say it.

We all sat there at the bar attempting to think of a next move.

"I wonder," said Jerry, "if I killed him?"

"Killed him how?" I asked.

"By mixing water with his vodka. He always drank it straight. It might have been the water that killed him."

"It might have," I said.

Then I motioned to the barkeep. "Tony," I said, "will you please serve the plump little lady a vodka and water?" Grace didn't think that was very humorous.

I didn't see it happen, but the way I heard it afterwards, Grace left and went to Wilbur's house and started beating on the door, beating and screaming and beating, and the brother, the doctor, came to the door but he wouldn't let her in, he was bereaved and drugged and he wouldn't let her in but Grace wouldn't quit. The doctor didn't know Grace very well (maybe he should have for she was a fine fuck) and he went to the phone and the police came but she was wild and crazed and it took two of them to put the bracelets on her. They made a mistake and had her hands in front and she came up and then down with the handcuffs and raked open one of the cop's cheeks, opened him up, so that you could look into the side of his head and see his teeth. More cops came and they took Grace away, screaming and kicking, and after that none of us ever saw her or each other again.

36

Rows AND ROWS of silent bicycles. Bins filled with bicycle parts. Rows and rows of bicycles hanging from the ceiling: green bikes, red bikes, yellow bikes, purple bikes, blue bikes, girls' bikes, boys' bikes, all hanging up there; the glistening spokes, the wheels, the rubber tires, the paint, the leather seats, tailights, headlights, handbrakes; hundreds of bicycles, row after row.

We got an hour for lunch. I'd eat quickly, having been up most of the night and early morning, I'd be tired, aching all over, and I found this secluded spot under the bicycles. I'd crawl down there, under three deep tiers of bicycles immaculately arranged. I'd lay there on my back, and suspended over me, precisely lined up, hung rows of gleaming silver spokes, wheel rims, black rubber tires, shiny new paint, everything in perfect order. It was grand, correct, orderly—500 or 600 bicycles stretching out over me, covering me, all in place. Somehow it was meaningful. I'd look up at them and know I had forty-five minutes of rest under the bicycle tree.

Yet I also knew with another part of me, that if I ever let go and dropped into the flow of those shiny new bicycles, I was done, finished, that I'd never be able to make it. So I just lay back and let the wheels and the spokes and the colors soothe me.

A man with a hangover should never lay flat on his back looking up at the roof of a warehouse. The wooden girders finally get to you; and the skylights—you can see the chicken wire in the glass skylights—that wire somehow reminds a man of jail. Then there's the heaviness of the eyes, the longing for just one drink, and then the sound of people moving about, you hear them, you know your hour is up, somehow you have to get on your feet and walk around and fill and pack orders . . .

37

SHE WAS THE manager's secretary. Her name was Carmen—but despite the Spanish name she was a blonde and she wore tight knitted dresses, high spiked heels, nylons, garter belt, her mouth was thick with lipstick, but, oh, she could shimmy, she could shake, she wobbled while bringing the orders up to the desk, she wobbled back to the office, all the boys watching every move, every twitch of her buttocks; wobbling, wiggling, wagging. I am not a lady's man. I never have been. To be a lady's man you have to make with the sweet talk. I've never been good at sweet talk. But, finally, with Carmen pressing me, I led her into one of the boxcars we were unloading at the rear of the warehouse and I took her standing up in the back of one of those boxcars. It was good, it was warm; I thought of blue sky and wide clean beaches, yet it was sad—there was definitely a lack of human feeling that I couldn't understand or deal with. I had that knit dress up around her hips and I stood there pumping it to her, finally pressing my mouth to her heavy mouth thick with scarlet lipstick and I came between two unopened cartons with the air full of cinders and with her back pressed against the filthy splintering boxcar wall in the merciful dark.

38

WE ALL DOUBLED up as both stock and shipping clerks. We each filled and shipped our own orders. Management was all for pinpointing errors. And since only one man was responsible for each order from start to finish, there was no way to pass the buck. Three or four goofed up orders and you were out.

Bums and indolents, all of us working there realized our days were numbered. So we relaxed and waited for them to find out how inept we were. Meanwhile, we lived with the system, gave them a few honest hours, and drank together at night.

There were three of us. Me. And a guy called Hector Gonzalves—tall, stooped, placid. He had a lovely Mexican wife who lived with him in a large double bed on upper Hill Street. I know because I went out with him one night and we drank beer and I frightened Hector's wife. Hector and I had walked in after a drunken evening in the bars and I pulled her out of bed and kissed her in front of Hector. I figured I could out-duke him. All I had to do was to keep an eye out for the steel. I finally apologized to both of them for being such an asshole. I could hardly blame her then for not warming to me and I never went back.

The third was Alabam, a small-time thief. He stole rear-view mirrors, screws and bolts, screwdrivers, light bulbs, reflectors, horns, batteries. He stole womens' panties and bedsheets off of clotheslines, rugs out of hallways. He'd go to the markets and buy a bag of potatos, but at the bottom of the sack he'd have steaks, slices of ham, cans of anchovies. He went by the name of George Fellows. George had a nasty habit: he'd drink with me and when I was almost to the point of helplessness, he'd attack me. He wanted badly to whip my ass but he was a thin fellow and cowardly to boot. I always managed to rouse myself enough to give him a few to the gut and the side of the head which would send him bounding and staggering down the stairway, usually with some small stolen item in his pocket—my washrag, a can opener, an alarm clock, my pen, a can of pepper, or perhaps a pair of scissors.

The manager of the bike warehouse, Mr. Hansen, was red-faced, sombre, green-tongued from sucking Clorets to get the whiskey off his breath. One day he called me into the office.

"Listen, Henry, those two boys are pretty dumb, aren't they?"

"They're all right."

"But, I mean, Hector especially . . . he *is* dumb, really. Oh, I mean, he's *all right*, but I mean, do you think he'll ever make it?"

"Hector is all right, sir."

"You mean it?"

"Of course."

"That Alabam. He's got weasel-eyes. He probably steals six dozen bike pedals a month, don't you think?"

"I don't think so, sir. I've never seen him take anything."

"Chinaski?"

"Yes, sir?"

"I'm giving you a ten dollar a week raise."

"Thank you, sir." We shook hands. That's when I realized that he and Alabam were in cahoots and splitting it right down the middle.

39

JAN WAS AN excellent fuck. She'd had two children but she was a most excellent fuck. We had met at an open air lunch counter—I was spending my last fifty cents on a greasy hamburger—and we struck up a conversation. She bought me a beer, gave me her phone number, and three days later I moved in to her apartment.

She had a tight pussy and she took it like it was a knife that was killing her. She reminded me of a butterfat little piglet. There was enough meanness and hostility in her to make me feel that with each thrust I was paying her back for her ill-temper. She'd had one ovary removed and claimed that she couldn't get pregnant; for only one ovary she responded generously.

Jan looked a lot like Laura—only she was leaner and prettier, with shoulder length blonde hair and blue eyes. She was strange; she was always hot in the morning with her hangovers. I was not so hot in the mornings with mine. I was a night man. But at night she was always screaming and throwing things at me: telephones, telephone books, bottles, glasses (full and empty), radios, purses, guitars, ashtrays, dictionaries, broken watch bands, alarm clocks ... She was an unusual woman. But one thing I could always count on, she wanted to fuck in the mornings, very much. And I had my bicycle warehouse.

Watching the clock on a typical morning, I'd give her the first one, me gagging and spewing just a bit, trying to hide it; then getting heated, coming, rolling off. "There, now," I'd say, "I'm going to be fifteen minutes late." And she'd trot off to the bathroom, happy as a bird, clean herself, poop, look at the hair under her arms, look in the mirror, worry more about age than death, then trot and get between the sheets again as I climbed into my stained shorts, to the noise of the traffic outside on Third Street, rolling east.

"Come on back to bed, daddy," she'd say.

"Look, I just got a ten dollar raise."

"We don't have to do anything. Just lay down here beside me."

"Oh shit, kid."

"Please! Just five minutes."

"Oh, fuck."

I'd get back in. She'd pull the covers back and grab my balls. Then she'd grab my penis. "Oh, he's *so* cute!"

I'd be thinking, I wonder when I can get out of here?

"Can I ask you something?"

"Go ahead."

"Do you mind if I kiss him?"

"No."

I heard and felt the kisses, then felt little licks. Then I forgot all about the bicycle warehouse. Then I heard her ripping up a newspaper. I felt something being fitted over the tip of my dick. "Look," she said.

I sat up. Jan had fashioned a little paper hat and fitted it over the head of my dick. Around the brim was a little yellow ribbon. The thing stood fairly tall.

"Oh, isn't he *cute?*" she asked me.

"*He?* That's *me*."

"Oh no, that isn't you, that's *him*, you have nothing to do with him."

"I don't?"

"No. Do you mind if I kiss him again?"

"All right, it's all right. Go ahead."

Jan lifted the hat off and holding on with one hand she began kissing where the hat had been. Her eyes looked deep into mine. The tip of it entered her mouth. I fell back, damned.

40

I ARRIVED AT the bicycle warehouse at 10:30 a.m. Starting time was 8. It was morning break time and the coffee wagon was outside. The warehouse crew was out there. I walked up and ordered a coffee, large, and a jelly dough-nut. I talked to Carmen, the manager's secretary, of boxcar fame. As usual Carmen was wearing a very tight knitted dress that fit her like a balloon fits the trapped air, maybe tighter. She had on layers and layers of dark red lipstick and while she talked she stood as close as possible, looking into my eyes and giggling, brushing parts of her body against me. Carmen was so aggressive that she was frightening, you wanted to run away from the pressure. Like most women, she wanted what she couldn't have any longer and Jan was draining all my semen and then some. Carmen thought I was playing sophisticated and hard to get. I leaned back clutching my jelly doughnut and she leaned into me. The break ended and we all walked inside. I visualized Carmen's lightly shit-stained panties draped over one of my toes as we lay in bed together in her shack on Main Street. Mr. Hansen, the manager, was standing outside his office: "Chinaski," he barked. I knew the sound: it was over for me.

I walked toward him and stood there. He was in a newly-pressed light tan summer suit, bow tie (green), tan shirt, with his black-and-tan shoes exquisitely shined. I was suddenly conscious of the nails in the soles of my scruffy shoes pressing up into the soles of my feet. Three buttons on my dirty shirt were missing. The zipper in my pants was jammed at half mast. My belt buckle was broken.

"Yes?" I asked.

"I'm going to have to let you go."

"O.K."

"You're a damned good clerk but I'm going to have to let you go."

I was embarrassed for him.

"You've been showing up for work at 10:30 for 5 or 6 days now. How do you think the other workers feel about this? They work an eight hour day."

"It's all right. Relax."

"Listen, when I was a kid I was a tough guy too. I used to show up for work with a black eye three or four times a month. But I made it into the job every day. On time. I worked my way up."

I didn't answer.

"What's wrong? How come you can't get in here on time?"

I had a sudden hunch that I might save my job if I gave him the right answer. "I just got married. You know how

69

it is. I'm on my honeymoon. In the mornings I start getting into my clothes, the sun is shining through the blinds, and she drags me down onto the mattress for one last fling of turkeyneck."

It didn't work. "I'll have them make out your severance check." Hansen strode toward his office. He went inside and I heard him say something to Carmen. I had another sudden inspiration and I knocked on one of the glass panels. Hansen looked up, walked over, slid back the glass.

"Listen," I said, "I never made it with Carmen. Honest. She's nice, but she's not my type. Make out my check for the whole week."

Hansen turned back into the office. "Make out his check for a week." It was only Tuesday. I hadn't expected that—but then he and Alabam were splitting 20,000 bicycle pedals down the middle. Carmen walked up and handed me the check. She stood there and gave me an indifferent smile as Hansen sat down at the telephone and dialed the State Employment Office.

41

I STILL HAD my thirty-five dollar car. The horses were hot. We were hot. Jan and I knew nothing about horses, but we lucked out. In those days they carded eight races instead of nine. We had a magic formula—it was called "Harmatz in the eighth." Willie Harmatz was a better than average jock, but he had weight problems, like Howard Grant does now. Examining the charts we noticed that Harmatz usually jumped one in on the last race, usually at a good price.

We didn't go out there every day. Some mornings we were just too sick from drinking to get out of bed. Then we'd get up in the early afternoon, stop off at the liquor store, stop off for an hour or two at some bar, listen to the juke box, watch the drunks, smoke, listen to the dead laughter—it was a nice way to go.

We were lucky. We only seemed to end up at the track on the right days. "Now look," I'd tell Jan, "He isn't going to do it again . . . it's impossible."

And there would come Willie Harmatz, with the old stretch run, looming up at the last moment through the gloom and the booze—there would come good old Willie at 16 to one, at 8 to one, at 9 to two. Willie kept saving us long after the rest of the world had become indifferent and had quit.

The thirty-five dollar car nearly always started, that wasn't the problem; the problem was to turn the headlights on. It was always very dark after the eighth race. Jan usually insisted upon taking a bottle of port in her purse. Then we drank beer at the track and—if things were going well—we drank at the track bar, mostly scotch and water. I already had one drunk driving rap and I'd find myself driving along in a car without headlights, hardly knowing where I was.

"Don't worry, baby," I'd say, "the next hard bump we hit will turn the lights on." We had the advantage of broken springs.

"Here's a dip! Hold your hat!"

"I don't have a hat!"

I'd floor it.

POW! POW! POW!

Jan would bounce up and down, trying to hold on to her bottle of port. I'd grip the wheel and look for a bit of light on the road ahead. Hitting those bumps would always turn the lights on. Sometimes sooner, sometimes later, but we'd always get the lights on.

42

WE LIVED ON the fourth floor of an old apartment house; we had two rooms in the back. The apartment was built at the edge of a high cliff so that when you looked out the back window it seemed as if you were twelve floors up instead of four. It was very much like living on the edge of the world—a last resting place before the final big drop.

Meanwhile, our winning streak at the track had ended, as all winning streaks end. There was very little money and we were drinking wine. Port and muscatel. We had the kitchen floor lined with gallon jugs of wine, six or seven of them, and in front of them were four or five fifths, and in front of the fifths were lined up three or four pints.

"Someday," I told Jan, "when they demonstrate that the world has four dimensions instead of just three, a man will be able to go for a walk and just disappear. No burial, no tears, no illusions, no heaven or hell. People will be sitting around and they'll say, 'What happened to George?' And somebody will say, 'Well, I don't know. He said he was going out for a pack of cigarettes.'"

"Listen," said Jan, "what time is it? I want to know what time it is."

"Well, let's see, we set the clock by the radio at midnight last night. We know that it gains 35 minutes every hour. It says 7:30 p.m. right now but we know that's not right because it's not dark enough yet. O.K. That's 7 and one half hours. 7 times 35 minutes, that's 245 minutes. One half of 35 is 17 and one half. That gives us 252 and one half minutes. O.K., that's 4 hours and 42 and one half minutes we owe them so we set the clock back to 5:47. That's it 5:47. It's dinner time and we don't have anything to eat."

Our clock had been dropped and broken and I had fixed it. I took the back off and found something wrong with the main spring and the fly wheel. The only way I could get the clock to run again was to shorten and tighten the main spring. This affected the speed of the clock's hands; you could almost watch the minute hand moving.

"Let's open another jug of wine," said Jan.

We really had nothing to do but drink wine and make love.

We'd eaten everything there was to eat. At night we took walks and stole cigarettes off dashboards and out of the glove compartments of parked cars.

"Should I make some pancakes?" asked Jan.

"I don't know if I can get another one of them down."

We were out of butter and lard so Jan fried the pancakes dry. And it wasn't pancake batter—it was flour mixed with water. They came out crisp. Real crisp.

"What kind of a man am I?" I wondered aloud. "My father told me I'd end up like this! Surely I can go out and get something? I'm *going* to go out and get something . . . But first, a good drink."

I filled a water glass full of port wine. It was vile tasting stuff and you couldn't think about it while you drank it or you'd heave it right up. So I'd always run another film up there in the movie of my mind. I'd think of an old castle in Scotland covered with moss—drawbridges, blue water, trees, blue sky, cumulus clouds. Or, I'd think of a sexy lady pulling on a pair of silk stockings very very slowly. This time I ran the silk stockings film.

I got the wine down. "I'm going. Goodbye Jan."

"Goodbye, Henry."

I walked down the hall, down the four flights of stairs, very quietly past the manager's apartment (we were behind in the rent), and into the street. I walked down the hill. I was at Sixth and Union Streets. I crossed Sixth Street, walked east. There was a small market there. I walked past the market, then I turned and approached it again. The vegetable stand was out front. There were tomatoes, cucumbers, oranges, pineapples, and grapefruit out there. I stood looking at them. I looked into the store; one old guy in an apron. He was talking to a woman. I picked up a cucumber and stuck it in my pocket and walked off. I was about fifteen feet away when I heard:

"Hey, mister! MISTER! You come back with that CUCUMBER or I'm going to call the COPS! If you don't wanna go to JAIL you bring that CUCUMBER BACK!"

I turned and made the long walk back. There were three or four people watching. I pulled the cucumber out of my pocket and put it back on top of the stack of cucumbers. Then I walked west. I walked up Union Street, up the west side of the hill, walked back up the four flights of stairs and opened the door. Jan looked up from her drink.

"I'm a failure," I said. "I couldn't even steal a cucumber."

"It's all right."

"Put the pancakes on."

I walked to the jug and poured another drink.

. . . I was riding a camel across the Sahara. I had a large nose, somewhat like an eagle's beak, but yet I was very handsome, yes, in white robes with green stripes. And I had courage, I had murdered more than one. I had a large curved sword at my belt. I rode toward the tent where a fourteen year old girl blessed with great wisdom and with an unpunctured hymen was eagerly waiting on a thick oriental carpet . . .

The drink went down; the poison shook my body; I could smell the flour and water burning. I poured a drink for Jan, I poured another drink for me.

AT SOME point during one of our hellish nights World War II ended. The war had always been at best a vague reality to me, but now it was over. And the jobs that had always been difficult to get became more so. I got up each morning and went to all the public employment agencies starting with the Farm Labor Market. I struggled up at 4:30 a.m., hungover, and was usually back before noon. I walked back and forth between the agencies, endlessly. Sometimes I did get an occasional day's work unloading a boxcar, but this was only after I started going to a private agency which took one third of my wages. Consequently, there was very little money and we fell further and further behind with the rent. But we kept the wine bottles lined up bravely, made love, fought, and waited.

When there was a little money we walked down to Grand Central Market to get cheap stew meat, carrots, potatoes, onions and celery. We'd put it all in a big pot and sit and talk, knowing we were going to eat, smelling it—the onions, the vegetables, the meat—listening to it bubble. We rolled cigarettes and went to bed together, and got up and sang songs. Sometimes the manager would come up and tell us to keep quiet, and remind us that we *were* behind with the rent. The tenants never complained about our fights but they didn't like our singing: *I Got Plenty Of Nothing*; *Old Man River*; *Buttons And Bows*; *Tumbling Along With The Tumbling Tumbleweeds*; *God Bless America*; *Deutschland über Alles*; *Bonaparte's Retreat*; *I Get The Blues When It Rains*; *Keep Your Sunny Side Up*; *No More Money In The Bank*; *Who's Afraid Of The Big Bad Wolf*; *When The Deep Purple Falls*; *A Tiskit A Tasket*; *I Married An Angel*; *Poor Little Lambs Gone Astray*; *I Want A Gal Just Like The Gal Who Married Dear Old Dad*; *How The Hell Ya Gonna Keep Them Down On The Farm*; *If I'd Known You Were Coming I'd A Baked A Cake* . . .

43

I was too sick one morning to get up at 4:30 a.m. —or according to our clock 7:27 and one half. I shut off the alarm and went back to sleep. A couple of hours later there was a loud noise in the hall. "What the hell is it?" asked Jan.

I got out of bed. I slept in my shorts. The shorts were stained—we wiped with newspapers that we crumpled and softened with our hands—and I often didn't get all of it cleaned off. My shorts were also ragged and had cigarette burns in them where the hot ashes had fallen in my lap.

I went to the door and opened it. There was thick smoke in the hall. Firemen in large metal helmets with numbers on them. Firemen dragging long thick hoses. Firemen dressed in asbestos. Firemen with axes. The noise and confusion was incredible. I closed the door.

"What is it?" asked Jan.

"It's the fire department."

"Oh," she said. She pulled the covers up over her head, rolled on her side. I got in beside her and slept.

44

I WAS FINALLY hired on at an auto parts warehouse. It was on Flower Street, down around Eleventh Street. They sold retail out the front and also wholesaled to other distributors and shops. I had to demean myself to get that one—I told them that I liked to think of my job as a second home. That pleased them.

I was the receiving clerk. I also walked to a half dozen places in the neighborhood and picked up parts. It did get me out of the building.

During my lunch period one day I noticed an intense and intelligent looking Chicano boy reading that day's entries in the newspaper.

"You play the horses?" I asked.

"Yeah."

"Can I see your paper?"

I looked down the entries. I handed the paper back.

"My Boy Bobby ought to take the eighth."

"I know it. And they don't even have him on top."

"All the better."

"What do you think he'll pay?"

"Around 9 to 2."

"I wish I could get a bet down."

"Me too."

"When's the last race go off at Hollywood Park?" he asked.

"5:30."

"We get out of here at 5:00."

"We'd never make it."

"We could try. My Boy Bobby's going to win."

"Just our luck."

"Want to come along?"

"Sure."

"Watch the clock. At 5:00 we'll cut out."

At five minutes to 5:00 we were both working as near the rear exit as possible. My friend, Manny, looked at his watch. "We'll steal two minutes. When I start running, follow me."

Manny stood there putting boxes of parts on a rear shelf. Suddenly he bolted. I was right behind him and we were out the rear door in a flash, then down the alley. He was a good runner. I found out afterwards that he had been an all-city quarter-miler in high school. I was four feet behind him all the way down the alley. His car was parked around the corner; he unlocked it and we were in and off.

"Manny, we'll never make it."

"We'll make it. I can tool this thing."

"We must be nine or ten miles away. We've got to get there, park, then get from the parking lot to the betting window."

"I can tool this thing. We'll make it."

"We can't stop for the red lights."

Manny had a fairly new car and he knew how to switch lanes. "I've played every track in this country."

"Caliente too?"

"Yes, Caliente. The bastards take twenty-five per cent."

"I know."

"It's worse in Germany. In Germany the take is fifty per cent."

"And they still get players?"

"They still get players. The suckers figure all they got to do is find the winner."

"We're bucking sixteen per cent, that's rough enough."

"Rough. But a good player can beat the take."

"Yes."

"Shit, a red light!"

"Fuck it. Go on through."

"I'm going to hang a right." Manny abruptly switched lanes and cut right at the signal. "Watch out for squad cars."

"Right." Manny could really tool that thing. If he could bet horses like he drove, Manny was a winner.

"You married, Manny?"

"No way."

"Women?"

"Sometimes. But it never lasts."

"What's the problem?"

"A woman is a full-time job. You have to choose your profession."

"I suppose there is an emotional drain."

"Physical too. They want to fuck night and day."

"Get one you like to fuck."

"Yes, but if you drink or gamble they think it's a put-down of their love."

"Get one who likes to drink, gamble and fuck."

"Who wants a woman like that?"

Then we were in the parking lot. Parking was free after the seventh race. Track admission also was free. Not having a program or a racing form was a problem, though. If there were any scratches you couldn't be sure which horse on the tote board was yours.

Manny locked the car. We started running. Manny opened up six lengths on me in the parking lot. We ran through an open gate and down into the tunnel. Manny held his six lengths through the tunnel, which at Hollywood Park is a long one. Coming out of the tunnel and into the track proper, I closed up on Manny until I was only five lengths back. I could see the horses at the gate. We sprinted toward the betting windows.

"My Boy Bobby . . . what's his number?" I yelled at a man with one leg as we ran past. Before he could answer I could no longer hear him. Manny ran toward the five dollar win window. When I got there he had his ticket. "What's his number?" "8! It's the 8 horse!" I got my $5 down and got the ticket as the bell rang shutting off the mutual machines and starting the horses out of the gate.

Bobby read 4 on the board off a 6 to one morning line. The 3 horse was the 6 to 5 favorite. It was an $8,000 claimer, a mile and one sixteenth. As they came around the first turn the favorite had a three-quarter length lead and Bobby was laying off his shoulder, like an executioner. He was loping loose and easy.

"We should have gone ten," I said. "We're in."

"Yeah, we've hooked the winner. We're in unless some big-ass closer comes out of the pack."

Bobby layed on the favorite's side halfway around the last turn and then made his move sooner than I expected. It was a trick jocks used sometimes. Bobby came around the favorite, dropped down on the rail and made his run right then instead of later. He had three and one half

79

lengths at the top of the stretch. Then out of the pack came the horse we had to beat, the 4 horse, he read 9 to one but he was coming. But Bobby was gliding. He won on a hand ride by two and one half lengths and paid $10.40.

45

THE NEXT DAY at work we were questioned about our sudden departure. We admitted we had made the last race and also that we were going again that afternoon. Manny had his horse picked and I had mine. Some of the guys asked if we would take bets out for them. I said that I didn't know. At noon Manny and I went to a bar for lunch.

"Hank, we take their bets."

"Those guys don't have any money—all they have is the coffee and chewing gum money their wives give them and we don't have time to mess around with the two dollar windows."

"We don't bet their money, we keep their money."

"Suppose they win?"

"They won't win. They always pick the wrong horse. They have a way of always picking the wrong horse."

"Suppose they bet our horse?"

"Then we know we've got the wrong horse."

"Manny, what are you doing working in auto parts?"

"Resting. My ambition is handicapped by laziness."

We had another beer and went back to the warehouse.

46

WE RAN THROUGH the tunnel as they were putting them in the gate. We wanted Happy Needles. We were only getting 9 to 5 and I figured we wouldn't win two days running, so I just bet $5. Manny went $10 win. Happy Needles won by a neck, getting up on the outside in the last few strides. We had that win and we also had $32 in bad bets, courtesy of the boys at the warehouse.

Word got around and the boys at other warehouses, where I went to pick up parts, placed their bets with me. Manny was right, there was seldom a payoff. They didn't know how to bet; they bet too short or too long and the price kept hitting in the middle. I bought a good pair of shoes, a new belt and two expensive shirts. The owner of the warehouse didn't look so powerful any more. Manny and I took a little longer with our lunches and came back smoking good cigars. But it was still a rough ride every afternoon to make the last race. The crowd got to know us as we came running out of that tunnel, and every afternoon they were waiting. They cheered and waved racing forms, and the cheers seemed to grow louder as we went past them on the dead run to the betting windows.

47

THE NEW LIFE didn't sit well with Jan. She was used to her four fucks a day and also used to seeing me poor and humble. After a day at the warehouse, then the wild ride and finally sprinting across the parking lot and down through the tunnel, there wasn't much love left in me. When I came in each evening she'd be well into her wine.

"Mr. Horseplayer," she'd say as I walked in. She'd be all dressed up; high-heels, nylons, legs crossed high, swinging her foot. "Mr. Big Horseplayer. You know, when I first met you I liked the way you walked across a room. You didn't just *walk* across a room, you walked like you were going to walk through a wall, like you owned everything, like nothing mattered. Now you got a few bucks in your pocket and you're not the same any more. You act like a dental student or a plumber."

"Don't give me any shit about plumbers, Jan."

"You haven't made love to me in two weeks."

"Love takes many forms. Mine has been more subtle."

"You haven't fucked me for two weeks."

"Have patience. In six months we'll be vacationing in Rome, in Paris."

"Look at you! Pouring yourself that good whiskey and letting me sit here drinking this cheap rot-gut wine."

I relaxed in a chair and swirled my whiskey around with the ice cubes. I had on an expensive yellow shirt, very loud, and I had on new pants, green with white pinstripes.

"Mr. Big-Time Horseplayer!"

"I give you soul. I give you wisdom and light and music and a bit of laughter. Also, I am the world's greatest horseplayer."

"Horse shit!"

"No, horseplayer." I drained my whiskey, got up, and made myself another.

48

THE ARGUMENTS WERE always the same. I understood it too well now—that great lovers were always men of leisure. I fucked better as a bum than as a puncher of timeclocks.

Jan began her counterattack, which was to argue with me, get me enraged and then run out into the streets, the bars. All she had to do was to sit on a barstool alone and the drinks, the offers would follow. I didn't think that was fair of her, naturally.

Most of the evenings fell into a pattern. She'd argue, grab her purse and be gone out the door. It was effective; we had lived and loved together for too many days. I had to feel it and feel it I did. But I always let her go as I sat helpless in my chair and drank my whiskey and tuned in the radio to a bit of classical music. I knew she was out there, and I knew there would be somebody else. Yet I had to let it happen, I had to let events take their own course.

This particular evening I sat there and something just broke in me, I could feel it breaking, something churned and rose in me and I got up and walked down the four flights of stairs and into the street. I walked down from Third and Union Streets to Sixth Street and then west along Sixth toward Alvarado. I walked along past the bars and I knew she was in one of them. I made a guess, walked in, and there was Jan sitting at the far end of the bar. She had a green and white silk scarf spread across her lap. She was sitting between a thin man with a large wart on his nose, and another man who was a little humped mound of a thing wearing bifocals and dressed in an old black suit.

Jan saw me coming. She lifted her head and even in the gloom of the bar she seemed to pale. I walked up behind her, standing near her stool. "I tried to make a woman out of you but you'll never be anything but a god damned whore!" I back-handed her and knocked her off her stool. She fell flat on the floor and screamed. I picked up her drink and finished it. Then I slowly walked toward the exit. When I got there I turned. "Now, if there's anybody here . . . who doesn't *like* what I just did . . . just say so."

There was no response. I guess they liked what I just did. I walked back out on Alvarado Street.

49

AT THE AUTO parts warehouse I did less and less. Mr. Mantz the owner would walk by and I would be crouched in a dark corner or in one of the aisles, very lazily putting incoming parts on the shelves.

"Chinaski, are you all right?"

"Yes."

"You're not sick?"

"No."

Then Mantz would walk off. The scene was repeated again and again with minor variations. Once he caught me making a sketch of the alley on the back of an invoice. My pockets were full of bookie money. The hangovers were not as bad, seeing as they were caused by the best whiskey money could buy.

I went on for two more weeks collecting paychecks. Then on a Wednesday morning Mantz stood in the center aisle near his office. He beckoned me forward with a motion of his hand. When I walked into his office, Mantz was back behind his desk. "Sit down, Chinaski." On the center of the desk was a check, face down. I slid the check face down along the glass top of the desk and without looking at it I slipped it in my wallet.

"You knew we were going to let you go?"

"Bosses are never hard to fathom."

"Chinaski, you haven't been pulling your weight for a month and you know it."

"A guy busts his damned ass and you don't appreciate it."

"You haven't been busting your ass, Chinaski."

I stared down at my shoes for some time. I didn't know what to say. Then I looked at him. "I've given you my *time*. It's all I've got to give—it's all any man has. And for a pitiful buck and a quarter an hour."

"Remember you begged for this job. You said your job was your second home."

". . . my time so that you can live in your big house on the hill and have all the things that go with it. If anybody has lost anything on this deal, on this arrangement . . . I've been the loser. Do you understand?"

"All right, Chinaski."

"All right?"

"Yes. Just go."

I stood up. Mantz was dressed in a conservative brown suit, white shirt, dark red necktie. I tried to finish it up with a flair. "Mantz, I want my unemployment insurance. I don't want any trouble about that. You guys are always trying to cheat a working man out of his rights. So don't give me any trouble or I'll be back to see you."

"You'll get your insurance. Now get the hell out of here!"

I got the hell out of there.

50

I HAD MY winnings and the bookie money and I just sat around and Jan liked that. After two weeks I was on unemployment and we relaxed and fucked and toured the bars and every week I'd go down to the California State Department of Employment and stand in line and get my nice little check. I only had to answer three questions:

"Are you able to work?"

"Are you willing to work?"

"Will you accept employment?"

"Yes! Yes! Yes!" I always said.

I also had to turn in a list of three companies where I had applied for work during the previous week. I took the names and addresses out of the phonebook. I was always surprised when one of the unemployment insurance applicants would answer "no" to any of the three questions. Their checks were immediately withheld and they were walked into another room where specially trained counselors would help send them on their way to skid row.

But in spite of the unemployment checks and the backlog of racetrack money, my bankroll began to vanish. Both Jan and I were totally irresponsible when we were drinking heavily and our troubles kept arriving by the carload. I was always running down to Lincoln Heights Jail to bail Jan out. She'd come down in the elevator with one of the dyke matrons at her elbow, almost always with either a black eye or a cut mouth and very often with a dose of the crabs, compliments of some maniac she'd met in a bar somewhere. Then there was bail money and then court costs and fines, plus a request by the judge to go to A.A. meetings for six months. I too gathered my share of suspended sentences and heavy fines. Jan managed to extricate me from a variety of charges ranging from attempted rape to assault to indecent exposure to being a public nuisance. Disturbing the peace was one of my favorites too. Most of these charges did not involve actually serving any time in jail—so long as the fines were paid. But it was a huge continual expense. I remember one night our old car stalled just outside of MacArthur Park. I looked into the rearview mirror and said, "O.K., Jan, we're in luck. We are going to get a push. He's coming up right behind us. There are some kind souls in this ugly world." Then I looked again: "Hold your ASS, Jan, he's going to HIT us!" The son of a bitch had never slackened speed and he hit us straight on from the rear, so hard that the front seat collapsed and we were thrown flat. I got out and asked the guy if he had learned to drive in China. I also threatened his life. The police arrived and asked me if I cared to blow up their little balloon. "Don't do it," said Jan. But I refused to listen. Somehow I had the idea that since the guy had been in the wrong in hitting us, that I couldn't possibly be intoxicated. The last I remember was getting into the squad car with Jan standing by our stalled car with the collapsed front seat. Incidents such as this—and they came along one after the other—cost us a lot of money. Little by little our lives were falling apart.

51

Jan and I were at Los Alamitos. It was Saturday. Quarter Horse Racing was a novelty then. You were a winner or a loser in eighteen seconds. At that time the grandstands consisted of row after row of simple unvarnished planks. It was getting crowded when we got there and we spread newspaper on our seats to show that they were taken. Then we went down to the bar to study our racing forms . . .

Along about the fourth race we were $18 ahead not counting expenses. We placed our bets for the next race and went back to our seats. A small gray-haired old man was sitting in the center of our newspapers. "Sir, those are our seats." "These seats aren't reserved." "I know these seats aren't reserved. But it's a matter of common courtesy. You see . . . some people get here early, poor people, like you and me, who can't afford reserved seats, and they lay newspapers down to indicate that the seats are taken. It's like a code, you know, a code of courtesy . . . because if the poor aren't decent to one another nobody else is going to be." "These seats are NOT reserved." He spread himself just a bit more on the newspapers we had placed there. "Jan, sit down. I'll stand." Jan tried to sit down. "Just move it a bit," I said, "if you can't be a gentleman, don't be a hog." He moved a little. I had the 7/2 shot in the outside post. He got bumped at the start and had to make a late run. He came on in the last second to hang a photo on the 6/5 favorite. I waited, hoping. They put up the other horse's number. I'd bet $20 win. "Let's get a drink." There was a tote board inside. The odds were up on the next race as we walked to the bar. We ordered drinks from a man who looked

*like a polar bear. Jan looked into the mirror worrying about the
sag in her cheeks and the pouches under her eyes. I never looked
into mirrors. Jan lifted her drink. "That old man in our seats,
he's got nerve. He's a spunky old dog." "I don't like him." "He
called your card." "What can a guy do with an old man?" "If
he had been young you wouldn't have done anything either." I
checked the tote. Three-Eyed Pete, reading 9/2, looked to be as
good as the first or second choice. We finished our drinks and I
went $5 win. When we got back to the stands, the old man was
still sitting there. Jan sat down next to him. Their legs were
pressed together. "What do you do for a living?" Jan asked him.
"Real estate. I make sixty thousand a year—after taxes." "Then
why don't you buy a reserved seat?" I asked. "That's my
prerogative." Jan pressed her flank against him. She smiled her
most beautiful smile. "You know," she said, "you've got the
nicest blue eyes?" "Uh huh." "What's your name?" "Tony
Endicott." "My name is Jan Meadows. My nickname is Misty."
They put the horses into the gate and they broke out. Three-Eyed
Pete got the first jump. He had a neck all the way. The last fifty
yards the boy got out the whip, spanking ass. The second favorite
made a tiny last lunge. They put up the photo again and I knew
that I had lost. "You got a cigarette?" Jan asked Endicott. He
handed it to Jan. She put it in her mouth, and with their flanks
pressed together, he lit her cigarette. They looked into each
other's eyes. I reached down and picked him up by the shirt collar.
He sagged a bit but I kept holding him up by his shirt collar.
"Sir, you are in my seat." "Yes. What are you going to do about
it?" "Look down between your feet. See the opening under your
seat? It's a thirty-five foot drop to the ground. I can push you
through." "You don't have the guts." They put up the second
favorite's number. I had lost. I got one of his legs down and
through, dangling. He struggled and was surprisingly strong. He
got his teeth into my left ear; he was biting my ear off. I got my
fingers around his throat and choked him. There was one long
white hair growing out of his throat. He gasped for air. His*

mouth opened and I pulled my ear out. I pushed his other leg through. A picture of Zsa Zsa Gabor flashed in my brain: she was cool, composed, immaculate, wearing pearls, her breasts bulging out of her low cut dress—then the lips that would never be mine said, no. The old man's fingers were clinging to a plank. He was hanging from the underside of the grandstand. I lifted one hand off. Then I lifted the other. He dropped through space. He fell slowly. He hit, bounced once, higher than one would expect, came down, hit again, took a second small bounce, then lay there motionless. There wasn't any blood. The people about us were very quiet. They bent over their racing forms. "Come on, let's go," I said. Jan and I walked out the side gate. People were still filing in. It was a mild afternoon, warm but not hot, gently warm. We walked outside past the track, past the clubhouse, and looking through the chain link fence at the east end we saw the horses come out of the stalls, making the slow circle to parade past the stands. We walked to the parking lot. We got into the car. We drove off. We drove back to the city: first past the oil wells and storage tanks, and then through open country past the small farms, quiet, neat, the stacked hay golden and ragged, the peeling white barns in the late afternoon sun, tiny farmhouses sitting in front on higher ground, perfect and warm. When we got to our apartment we found there was nothing to drink. I sent Jan out for something. When she came back we sat and drank, not saying much.

52

WHEN I AWAKENED I was sweating. Jan's leg was thrown across my belly. I moved it. Then I got up and went to the bathroom. I had the running shits.

I thought, well, I'm alive and I'm sitting here and nobody's bothering me.

Then I got up and wiped, looked; what a mess, I thought, what a lovely powerful stink. Then I vomited and flushed it all away. I was very pale. A chill convulsed my body, shaking me; then there was a rush of warmth, my neck and ears burned, my face reddened. I felt dizzy and closed my eyes and leaned on both hands over the washbowl. It passed.

I went and sat on the edge of the bed and rolled a cigarette. I hadn't wiped myself very well. When I got up to look for a beer there was a wet brown stain. I went into the bathroom and wiped myself again. Then I sat on the bed with my beer and waited for Jan to awaken.

I had first learned that I was an idiot in the school yard. I was taunted and poked at and jeered, as were the other one or two idiots. My only advantage over the other one or two, who were beaten and chasen, was that I was sullen. When surrounded I was not terrified. They never attacked me but would finally turn on one of the others and beat them as I watched.

Jan moved, then awakened and looked at me.

"You're awake."

"Yes."

"That was some night."

"Night? Hell, it's the *day* that bothers me."

"What do you mean?"

"You know what I mean."

Jan got up and went to the bathroom. I mixed her a port wine with icecubes and set it on the nightstand.

She came out, sat down and picked up the drink. "How do you feel?" she asked.

"Here I've killed a guy and you ask me how I feel."

"What guy?"

"You remember. You weren't that drunk. We were at Los Alamitos, I dropped the old guy through the grand-stand. Your blue-eyed would-be lover with $60,000 a year."

"You're crazy."

"Jan, you get on the booze, you black out. I do too, but you're worse than I am."

"We weren't at Los Alamitos yesterday. You hate quarter horses."

"I even remember the names of the horses I bet on."

"We sat here all day and evening yesterday. You told me about your parents. Your parents hated you. Right?"

"Right."

"So now you're a little crazy. No love. Everybody needs love. It's warped you."

"People don't need love. What they need is success in one form or another. It can be love but it needn't be."

"The Bible says, 'Love thy neighbor.'"

"That could mean to leave him alone. I'm going out to get a paper."

Jan yawned and lifted her breasts. They were an interesting brown-gold color—like tan mixed with dirt. "Get a little bottle of whiskey while you're out."

I dressed and walked down the hill toward Third Street. There was a drugstore at the bottom of the hill and a bar next to that. The sun was tired, and some of the cars went east and some of the cars went west, and it dawned on me that if everybody would only drive in the same direction everything would be solved.

I bought a newspaper. I stood there reading through it. There was no mention of a murdered horseplayer at Los Alamitos. Of course, it had happened in Orange County. Maybe Los Angeles County only reported their own murders.

I bought a half pint of Grand Dad at the liquor store and walked back up the hill. I folded the paper under my arm and opened the door to our place. I threw the half pint to Jan. "Ice, water and a good jolt for both of us. I am crazy."

Jan walked into the kitchen to mix the drinks and I sat down and opened the paper and turned to the race results at Los Alamitos. I read the result of the fifth race: Three-Eyed Pete had gone off at 9/2 and had been beaten by a nose by the second favorite.

When Jan brought the drink I drank it straight down. "You keep the car," I said, "and half the money I have left is yours."

"It's another woman, isn't it?"

"No."

I got all the money together and spread it out on the kitchen table. There was $312 and some change. I gave Jan the car key and $150.

"It's Mitzi, isn't it?"

"No."

"You don't love me anymore."

"Stop the shit, will you?"

"You're tired of fucking me, aren't you?"

"Just drive me down to Greyhound, will you?"

She went into the bathroom and started getting ready. She was sore. "You and I have lost it. It isn't like it was at the beginning."

I mixed myself another drink and didn't answer. Jan stepped out of the bathroom and looked at me. "Hank, stay with me."

"No."

She went back in and didn't say anything more. I got the suitcase out and began putting my few things in there. I took the clock. She wouldn't need it.

Jan left me outside the Greyhound bus depot. She hardly gave me time to lift my suitcase out and then she was gone. I walked in and purchased my ticket. Then I walked over and sat down on the hard-backed benches with the other passengers. We all sat there and looked at each other and didn't look at each other. We chewed gum, drank coffee, went into restrooms, urinated, slept. We sat on the hard benches and smoked cigarettes we didn't want to smoke.

We looked at each other and didn't like what we saw. We looked at the things on the counters and display racks: potato chips, magazines, peanuts, best sellers, chewing gum, breath-chasers, licorice drops, toy whistles.

53

MIAMI WAS AS far as I could go without leaving the country. I took Henry Miller with me and tried to read him all the way across. He was good when he was good, and vice versa. I had a pint. Then I had another pint, and another. The trip took four days and five nights. Outside of a leg-and-thigh rubbing episode with a young brunette girl whose parents would no longer support her in college, nothing much happened. She got off in the middle of the night in a particularly barren and cold part of the country, and vanished. I had always had insomnia and the only time I could really sleep on a bus was when I was totally drunk. I didn't dare try that. When we arrived I hadn't slept or shit for five days and I could barely walk. It was early evening. It felt good to be in the streets again.

ROOMS FOR RENT. I walked up and rang the doorbell. At such times one always places the old suitcase out of the view of the person who will open the door.

"I'm looking for a room. How much is it?"

"$6.50 a week."

"May I look at it?"

"Surely."

I walked in and followed her up the stairway. She was about forty-five but her behind swayed nicely. I have followed so many women up stairways like that, always thinking, if only some nice lady like this one would offer to take care of me and feed me warm tasty food and lay out clean stockings and shorts for me to wear, I would accept.

She opened the door and I looked in.

"All right," I said, "it looks all right."

"Are you employed?"

"Self-employed."

"May I ask what you do?"

"I'm a writer."

"Oh, have you written books?"

"Oh, I'm hardly ready for a novel. I just do articles, bits for magazines. Not very good really but I'm developing."

"All right. I'll give you your key and make out a receipt."

I followed her down the stairway. The ass didn't sway as nicely going down the stairway as going up. I looked at the back of her neck and imagined kissing her behind the ears.

"I'm Mrs. Adams," she said. "Your name?"

"Henry Chinaski."

As she made out the receipt, I heard sounds like the sawing of wood coming from behind the door to our left—only the rasps were punctuated with gasps for breath. Each breath seemed to be the last yet each breath finally led painfully to another.

"My husband is ill," said Mrs. Adams as she handed me the receipt and my key, she smiled. Her eyes were a lovely hazel color and sparkled. I turned and walked back up the stairs.

When I got into my room I remembered I had left my suitcase downstairs. I went down to fetch it. As I walked past Mrs. Adams' door the gasping sounds were much louder. I took my suitcase upstairs, threw it on the bed, then walked downstairs again and out into the night. I found a main boulevard a little to the north, walked into a grocery store and bought a jar of peanut butter and a loaf of bread. I had a pocket knife and would be able to spread the peanut butter on the bread and have something to eat.

When I got back to the roominghouse I stood in the hall and listened to Mr. Adams, and I thought, that's Death. Then I went up to my room and opened the jar of peanut butter and while listening to the death sounds from below I dug my fingers in. I ate it right off my fingers. It was great. Then I opened the bread. It was green and moldy and had a sharp sour smell. How could they sell bread like that? What kind of a place was Florida? I threw the bread on the floor, got undressed, turned out the light, pulled up the covers and lay there in the dark, listening.

54

IN THE MORNING it was very quiet and I thought, that's nice, they've taken him to the hospital or the morgue. Now maybe I'll be able to shit. I got dressed and went down the hallway to the bathroom and sure enough I did. Then I walked down to my room, got into bed and slept some more.

I was awakened by a knock on the door. I sat up and called, "Come in!" before I thought. It was a lady dressed entirely in green. The blouse was low-cut, the skirt was very tight. She looked like a movie star. She simply stood there looking at me for some time. I was sitting up, in my shorts, holding the blanket in front of me. Chinaski the great lover. If I was any kind of man, I thought, I would rape her, set her panties on fire, force her to follow me all over the world, make tears come to her eyes with my love letters written on light red tissue paper. Her features were indefinite, not at all like her body; there was the general round shape of her face, the eyes seemed to be searching mine but her hair was a bit messy and uncombed. She was in her mid-thirties. Something, however, was exciting her. "Mrs. Adams' husband died last night," she said. "Ah," I said, wondering if she felt as good about the noise stopping as I did.

"And we're taking up a collection to buy flowers for Mr. Adams' funeral."

"I don't think that flowers are meant for the dead who don't need them," I said rather lamely.

She hesitated. "We thought it would be a nice thing to do and I wondered if you would like to contribute?"

"I'd like to but I just arrived in Miami last night and I'm broke."

"Broke?"

"Looking for a job. I'm up against it, as they say. I've spent my last dime on a jar of peanut butter and a loaf of bread. The bread was green, greener than your dress. I left it on the floor there and even the rats didn't touch it."

"Rats?"

"I don't know about your room."

"But when I talked to Mrs. Adams last evening I asked her about the new roomer—we're all kind of like a family here—and she said that you were a writer, that you wrote for magazines like *Esquire* and *Atlantic Monthly*."

"Hell, I can't write. That's just conversation. It makes the landlady feel better. What I need is a job, any kind of job."

"Can't you contribute twenty-five cents? Twenty-five cents wouldn't hurt you."

"Honey, I need the twenty-five cents more than Mr. Adams does."

"Honor the dead, young man."

"Why not honor the living? I'm lonely and desperate and you look very lovely in your green dress."

She turned, walked out, walked down the hall, opened the door to her room, went in, closed the door, and I never saw her again.

55

THE FLORIDA STATE Department of Employment was a pleasant place. It wasn't as crowded as the Los Angeles office which was always full. It was my turn for a little good luck, not much, but a little. It was true that I didn't have much ambition, but there ought to be a place for people without ambition, I mean a better place than the one usually reserved. How in the hell could a man enjoy being awakened at 6:30 a.m. by an alarm clock, leap out of bed, dress, force-feed, shit, piss, brush teeth and hair, and fight traffic to get to a place where essentially you made lots of money for somebody else and were asked to be grateful for the opportunity to do so?

My name was called. The clerk had my card in front of him, the one I had filled out when entering. I had elaborated on my work experience in a creative way. Pros do that: you leave out the previous low-grade jobs and describe the better ones fully, also leaving out any mention of those blank stretches when you were alcoholic for six months and shacked with some woman just released from a madhouse or a bad marriage. Of course, since all my previous jobs were low-grade I left out the lower low-grade.

The clerk ran his fingers through his little card file. He pulled one out. "Ah, here's a job for you."

"Yes?"

He looked up. "Sanitation Worker."

"What?"

"Garbage man."

"I don't want it."

I shuddered at the thought of all that garbage, the morning hangovers, blacks laughing at me, the impossible weight of the cans, and me pukeing my guts into the orange rinds, coffee grounds, wet cigarette ashes, banana peels and the used tampax.

"What's the matter? Not good enough for you? It's 40 hours. And security. A lifetime of security."

"You take that job and I'll take yours."

Silence.

"I'm trained for this job."

"Are you? I spent two years in college. Is that a prerequisite to pick up garbage?"

"Well, what kind of job do you want?"

"Just keep flipping through your cards."

He flipped through his cards. Then he looked up. "We have nothing for you." He stamped the little book they'd given me and handed it back. "Contact us in seven days for further employment possibilities."

56

I FOUND A job through the newspaper. I was hired by a clothing store but it wasn't in Miami it was in Miami Beach, and I had to take my hangover across the water each morning. The bus ran along a very narrow strip of cement that stood up out of the water with no guard-rail, no nothing; that's all there was to it. The bus driver leaned back and we roared along over this narrow cement strip surrounded by water and all the people in the bus, the twenty-five or forty or fifty-two people trusted him, but I never did. Sometimes it was a new driver, and I thought, how do they select these sons of bitches? There's deep water on both sides of us and with one error of judgement he'll kill us all. It was ridiculous. Suppose he had an argument with his wife that morning? Or cancer? Or visions of God? Bad teeth? Anything. He could do it. Dump us all. I knew that if I was driving that *I* would consider the possibility or desirability of drowning everybody. And sometimes, after just such considerations, possibility turns into reality. For each Joan of Arc there is a Hitler perched at the other end of the teeter-totter. The old story of good and evil. But none of the bus drivers ever dumped us. They were thinking instead of car payments, baseball scores, haircuts, vacations, enemas, family visits. There wasn't a real man in the whole shitload. I always got to work sick but safe. Which demonstrates why Schumann was more relative than Shostakovich . . .

I WAS hired as what they called the extra ball-bearing. The extra ball-bearing is the man who is simply turned loose without specific duties. He is supposed to *know* what to do after consulting some deep well of ancient instinct. Instinctively one is supposed to know what will best keep things running smoothly, best maintain the company, the Mother, and meet all her little needs which are irrational, continual and petty.

A good extra ball-bearing man is faceless, sexless, sacrificial; he is always waiting at the door when the first man with the key arrives. Soon he is hosing off the sidewalk, and he greets each person by name as they arrive, always with a bright smile and in a reassuring manner. Obeisant. That makes everybody feel a little better before the bloody grind begins. He sees that toilet paper is plentiful, especially in the ladies' crapper. That wastebaskets never overflow. That no grime coats the windows. That small repairs are promptly made on desks and office chairs. That doors open easily. That clocks are set. That carpeting remains tacked down. That overfed powerful women do not have to carry small packages.

I wasn't very good. My idea was to wander about doing nothing, always avoiding the boss, and avoiding the stoolies who might report to the boss. I wasn't all that clever. It was more instinct than anything else. I always started a job with the feeling that I'd soon quit or be fired, and this gave me a relaxed manner that was mistaken for intelligence or some secret power.

It was a completely self-sufficient, self-contained clothing store, factory and retail business combined. The showroom, the finished product and the salesmen were all downstairs, and the factory was up above. The factory was a maze of catwalks and runways that even the rats couldn't crawl, long narrow lofts with men and women sitting and working under thirty watt bulbs, squinting, treading pedals, threading needles, never looking up or speaking, bent and quiet, doing it.

At one time one of my jobs in New York City had been to take bolts of fabric up to lofts like this. I would roll my hand truck in the busy street, pushing it through traffic, then into an alley behind some grimy building. There would be a dark elevator and I'd have to pull on ropes with stained round wooden spools attached. One rope meant up, another rope signalled down. There was no light and as the elevator climbed slowly I'd watch in the dark for white numbers written on the bare walls—3, 7, 9, scrawled in chalk by some forgotten hand. I'd reach my floor, tug on another rope with my fingers and using all my strength slowly slide open the heavy old metal door, revealing row upon row of old Jewish ladies at their machines, laboring over piecework; the number one seamstress at the #1 machine, bent on maintaining her place; the number two girl at the #2 machine, ready to replace her should she falter. They never looked up or in any way acknowledged my presence as I entered.

In this clothing factory and store in Miami Beach, no deliveries were necessary. Everything was on hand. My first day I walked around the maze of lofts looking at people. Unlike New York, most of the workers were black. I walked up to a black man, quite small—almost tiny, who had a more pleasant face than most. He was doing some close work with a needle. I had a half pint in my pocket. "You got a rotten job there. Care for a drink?"

"Sure," he said. He took a good hit. Then handed the bottle back. He offered me a cigarette. "You new in town?" "Yeah." "Where you from?" "Los Angeles." "Movie star?" "Yes, on vacation." "You shouldn't be talking to the help." "I know." He fell silent. He looked like a little monkey, an old graceful monkey. For the boys downstairs, he *was* a monkey. I took a hit. I was feeling good. I watched them all working quietly under their thirty watt bulbs, their hands moving delicately and swiftly. "My name's Henry," I said. "Brad," he answered. "Listen, Brad, I get the deep deep blues watching you people work. Suppose I sing you guys and gals a little song?" "Don't." "You've got a rotten job there. Why do you do it?" "Shit, ain't no other way." "The Lord said there was." "You believe in the Lord?" "No." "What do you believe in?" "Nothing." "We're even."

I talked to some of the others. The men were uncommunicative, some of the women laughed at me. "I'm a spy," I laughed back. "I'm a company spy. I'm watching everybody."

I took another hit. Then I sang them my favorite song, "My Heart is a Hobo." They kept working. Nobody looked up. When I finished they were still working. It was quiet for some time. Then I heard a voice: "Look, white boy, don't come down on us."

I decided to go hose off the front sidewalk.

57

I DON'T KNOW how many weeks I worked there. I think six. At one point I was transferred to the receiving section, checking incoming shipments of trousers against the packing lists. These were orders being returned for credit from branch stores, usually out of the state. The packing lists were never wrong probably because the guy at the other end was too frightened for his job to be careless. Usually he is on the seventh of thirty-six payments for his new car, his wife is taking a ceramics class on Monday night, the interest on his mortgage is eating him alive, and each one of his five kids drinks a quart of milk a day.

You know, I'm not a clothes man. Clothes bore me. They are terrible things, cons, like vitamins, astrology, pizzas, skating rinks, pop music, heavyweight championship fights, etc. I was sitting there pretending to count the incoming pants when suddenly I came across something special. There was electricity in the fabric, it clung to my fingers and would not let go. Somebody had finally done something interesting. I examined the fabric. It looked as magical as it felt.

I got up, took the pants with me to the crapper. I went inside, locked the door. I had never stolen anything.

I took my own pants off, flushed the toilet. Then I put the magic pants on. I rolled the magic pantlegs up to just below my knees. Then I put my own pants back over them.

I flushed the toilet again.

Then I walked out. In my nervousness it seemed as if everyone was staring at me. I walked to the front of the store. It was about one and one half hours before quitting time. The boss was standing at a counter near the door. He stared at me. "I have something to take care of, Mr. Silverstein. Just dock my pay . . ."

58

I GOT TO MY room and took my old pants off. I rolled down the legs of my magic pants, put on a clean shirt, shined my shoes, and walked back out on the street in my new pants. They were a rich brown color, with fancy piping running vertically in the cloth.

The fabric glowed. I stood on the corner and lit a cigarette. A cab pulled up. The driver stuck his head out the window: "Taxi, sir?" "No thanks," I said, tossing the match into the gutter and crossing the street.

I walked around for fifteen or twenty minutes. Three or four cabbies asked me if I wanted a ride. Then I bought a bottle of port and went back to my place. I took my clothes off, hung them up, went to bed, drank the wine and wrote a short story about a poor clerk who worked in a clothing factory in Miami. This poor clerk met a rich society girl on the beach one day during his lunch hour. He deserved her money and she did everything in her power to show that she deserved him . . .

When I arrived for work in the morning, Mr. Silverstein was standing in front of the counter near the door. He had a check in his hand. He moved the hand toward me. I stepped forward and took the check. Then I walked back out on the street.

59

IT TOOK FOUR days and five nights for the bus to reach Los Angeles. As usual I neither slept nor defecated during the trip. There was some minor excitement when a big blonde got on somewhere in Louisiana. That night she started selling it for $2, and every man and one woman on the bus took advantage of her generosity except me and the bus driver. Business was transacted at night in the back of the bus. Her name was Vera. She wore purple lipstick and laughed a lot. She approached me during a brief stop in a coffee and sandwich shop. She stood behind me and asked,

"Whatsa matter, you too good for me?" I didn't reply. "A fag," I heard her mutter disgustedly as she sat down next to one of the regular guys . . .

In Los Angeles I toured the bars in our old neighborhood looking for Jan. I didn't get anywhere until I found Whitey Jackson working behind the bar in the Pink Mule. He told me that Jan was working as a chambermaid in the Durham Hotel at Beverly and Vermont. I walked on over. I was looking for the manager's office when she stepped out of a room. She looked good, like getting away from me for a while had helped her. Then she saw me. She just stood there, her eyes got very blue and round and she stood there. Then she said it, "Hank!" She rushed over and we were in each other's arms. She kissed me wildly, I tried to kiss back. "Jesus," she said, "I thought I'd never see you again!" "I'm back." "Are you back for good?" "L.A.'s my town." "Step back," she said, "let me look at you." I stepped back, grinning. "You're thin. You've lost weight," Jan said. "You're looking good," I said, "are you alone?" "Yes." "There's nobody?" "Nobody. You know I can't stand people." "I'm glad you're working." "Come to my room," she said.

I followed her. The room was very small but there was a good feel to it. You could look out the window and see the traffic, watch the signals working, see the paperboy on the corner. I liked the place. Jan threw herself on the bed. "Come on, lay down," she said. "I'm embarrassed." "I love you, you idiot," she said, "we've fucked 800 times, so relax." I took my shoes off and stretched out. She lifted a leg. "Still like my legs?" "Hell yes. Jan, have you finished your work?" "All but Mr. Clark's room. And Mr. Clark doesn't care. He leaves me tips." "Oh?" "I'm not doing anything. He just leaves tips." "Jan . . ." "Yes?" "The bus fare took all my money. I need a place to stay until I find a job." "I can hide you here." "Can you?" "Sure." "I love you, baby," I said. "Bastard," she said. We began to go at it. It felt good. It felt very very good.

Afterwards Jan got up and opened a bottle of wine. I opened my last pack of cigarettes and we sat in bed drinking and smoking. "You're all there," she said. "What do you mean?" "I mean, I never met a man like you." "Oh yeah?" "The others are only ten per cent there or twenty per cent, you're all there, *all* of you is very there, it's so different." "I don't know anything about it." "You're a hooker, you can hook women." That made me feel good. After we finished our cigarettes we made love again. Then Jan sent me out for another bottle. I came back. I had to.

60

I GOT HIRED immediately at a fluorescent light fixture company. It was up on Alameda Street, to the north, in a cluster of warehouses. I was the shipping clerk. It was quite easy, I took the orders out of a wire basket, filled them, packed the fixtures in cartons, and stacked the cartons on skids out on the loading dock, each carton labeled and numbered. I weighed the cartons, made out a bill of lading, and phoned the trucking companies to come pick the stuff up.

The first day I was there, in the afternoon, I heard a loud crash behind me near the assembly line. The old wooden racks that housed the finished parts were pulling away from the wall and crashing to the floor—metal and glass were hitting the cement floor, smashing, making a terrible racket. The assembly line workers ran to the other side of the building. Then it was silent. The boss, Mannie Feldman, stepped out of the office.

"What the hell's going on here?"

Nobody answered.

"*All right, shut down the assembly line! Everybody get a hammer and nails and get those fucking racks back up there!*"

Mr. Feldman walked back into his office. There was nothing for me to do but to get in and help them. None of us were carpenters. It took us all afternoon and half the next morning to nail the racks back up. As we finished Mr. Feldman walked out of his office.

"*So, you did it? All right, now listen to me—I want the 939's stacked on top, the 820's next on down, and the louvers and glass on the bottom shelves, get it? Now, does everybody get it?*"

There wasn't any answer. The 939's were the heaviest fixtures—they were really heavy mothers—and he wanted them on top. He was the boss. We went about it. We stacked them up there, all that weight, and we stacked the light stuff on the bottom racks. Then we went back to work. Those racks held up the rest of the day and through the night. In the morning we began to hear creaking sounds. The racks were starting to go. The assembly line workers began to edge away, they were grinning. About ten minutes before the morning coffee break everything came down again. Mr. Feldman came running out of his office:

"*What the hell's going on here?*"

61

FELDMAN WAS TRYING to collect his insurance and go bankrupt at the same time. The next morning a dignified looking man came down from the Bank of America. He told us not to build any more racks. "Just stack that shit on the floor," was the way he put it. His name was Jennings, Curtis Jennings. Feldman owed the Bank of America a lot of money and the Bank of America wanted its money back before the business went under. Jennings took over management of the company. He walked around watching everybody. He went through Feldman's books; he checked the locks and the windows and the security fence around the parking lot. He came up to me: "Don't use Sieberling Truck Lines any more. They had four thefts while running one of your shipments through Arizona and New Mexico. Any particular reason you been using those boys?" "No, no reason." The agent from Sieberling had been slipping me ten cents for each five hundred pounds of freight shipped out.

Within three days Jennings fired a man who worked in the front office and replaced three men on the assembly line with three young Mexican girls willing to work for half the pay. He fired the janitor and, along with doing the shipping, had me driving the company truck on local deliveries.

I got my first paycheck and moved out of Jan's place and into an apartment of my own. When I came home one night, she had moved in with me. What the fuck, I told her, my land is your land. Shortly thereafter, we had our worst fight. She left and I got drunk for three days and three nights. When I sobered up I knew my job was gone. I never went back. I decided to clean up the apartment. I vacuumed the floors, scrubbed the window ledges, scoured the bathtub and sink, waxed the kitchen floor, killed all the spiders and roaches, emptied and washed the ashtrays, washed the dishes, scrubbed the kitchen sink, hung up clean towels and installed a new roll of toilet paper. I must be turning fag, I thought.

When Jan finally came home—a week later—she accused me of having had a woman here, because everything looked so clean. She acted very angry, but it was just a cover for her own guilt. I couldn't understand why I didn't get rid of her. She was compulsively unfaithful—

she'd go off with anyone she met in a bar, and the lower and the dirtier he was the better she liked it. She was continually using our arguments to justify herself. I kept telling myself that all the women in the world weren't whores, just mine.

62

I WALKED INTO the Times Building. I had taken two years of Journalism at Los Angeles City College. I was stopped at the desk by a young lady. "You need a reporter here?" I asked. She handed me a printed sheet of paper. "Please fill this out." It was the same at most newspapers in most cities. You were hired because you were famous or because you knew somebody. But I filled out the form. I made it look good. Then I left and walked down Spring Street.

It was a hot summer day. I began to sweat and itch. My crotch itched. I began to scratch. The itching became unbearable. I walked along scratching. I couldn't be a reporter, I couldn't be a writer, I couldn't find a good woman, all I could do was walk along and scratch like a monkey. I hurried to my car which I had parked on Bunker Hill. I drove back to the apartment in a hurry. Jan wasn't there. I went into the bathroom and stripped down.

I dug into my crotch with my fingers and I found something. I pulled it out. I dropped it into the palm of one hand and looked at it. It was white and had many tiny legs. It moved. It fascinated me. Then suddenly it leaped to the tile of the bathroom floor. I stared at it. With one quick leap it was gone. Probably back into my pubic hair! I felt sickened and angered. I stood there searching for it. I couldn't find it. My stomach quivered. I gagged into the toilet and dressed again.

The corner drugstore wasn't far. There was an old woman and an old man standing behind the counter. The woman came over. "No," I said, "I want to talk to him." "Oh," she said.

The old man walked over. He was the pharmacist. He looked very clean. "I'm the victim of an inequity," I told him.

"What?"

"Now look, do you have anything for . . ."

"For what?"

"Spiders, fleas . . . gnats, nits . . ."

"For what?"

"*Do you have anything for crabs?*"

The old man gave me a disgusted look. "Wait here," he said. He got something out from under the end of the counter. He came back and standing as far away from me as possible he handed me a little green and black cardboard box. I accepted it humbly. I handed him a $5 bill. I received my change at arm's length. The old woman had backed away into a corner of the drugstore. I felt like a holdup man.

"Wait," I said to the old man.

"What is it now?"

"I want some rubbers."

"How many?"

"Oh, a pack, a handful."

"Wet or dry?"

"What?"

"Wet or dry?"

"Give me the wet."

The old man gingerly handed me the rubbers. I handed him the money. Once again he handed me the change at arm's length. I walked out. As I walked down the street I took the rubbers out and looked at them. Then I threw them into the gutter.

Back at the apartment I stripped down and read the instructions. It said to apply the ointment to the invaded parts and wait thirty minutes. I turned the radio on, found a symphony, and squeezed the ointment out of the tube. It was green. I applied it thoroughly. Then I lay down on the bed and looked at the clock. Thirty minutes. Hell, I hated those crabs, I'd take an hour's worth. After forty-five minutes it started to burn. I'll kill every one of those fuckers, I thought. The burning increased. I rolled over on the bed and clenched my fists. I listened to Beethoven. I listened to Brahms, I hung on. I barely made the hour. I filled the tub and jumped in and washed the ointment off. When I got out of the tub I couldn't walk. The insides of my thighs were burned, my balls were burned, my belly was burned, I was a bright flaming red, I looked like an orangutang. I moved very slowly toward the bed. But I had killed the crabs, I had watched them go down the bathtub drain.

When Jan got home I was squirming on the bed. She stood looking at me. "What is it?" I rolled and cursed.

"You fucking whore! Look what you've *done* to me!"

I leaped up. I showed Jan the insides of my thighs, my belly, my balls. My balls dangled in red agony. My pecker was flaming.

"God! What is it?"

"Don't you know? Don't you know? *I* haven't fucked anybody else! I got it from YOU! You're a *carrier*, a disease ridden *slut!*"

"What?"

"The crabs, the crabs, you gave me the CRABS!"

"No, I don't have the crabs. Geraldine must have them."

"What?"

"I stayed with Geraldine, I must have gotten them sitting on Geraldine's toilet."

I threw myself down on the bed. "Oh, don't give me any

of that shit! Go get us something to drink! There's not a fucking thing to drink around here!"

"I don't have any money."

"Take it out of my wallet. You know how to do that. And hurry! Something to drink! I'm dying!"

Jan left. I could hear her running down the stairs. The radio now played Mahler.

63

I AWAKENED SICK the next morning. It had been nearly impossible to sleep with the sheet over me. The burns seemed a little better, however. I got up and vomited and looked at my face in the mirror. They had me. I didn't have a chance.

I lay back on the bed. Jan was snoring. She didn't snore loudly but her snoring was persistent. It was something like I'd imagine a small hog would snore. Almost snorts. I looked at her wondering who I had been living with. She had a small pug nose and her blonde hair was turning "mousey" as she described it, as it went gray. Her face was sagging, she was getting jowls, she was ten years older than I. It was only when she was made up and was dressed in a tight skirt and wearing high heels that she looked good. Her ass was still shapely as were her legs and she had a seductive wiggle when she walked. Now as I looked at her she didn't look so wonderful. She was sleeping partly on one side and her pot belly was hanging out. She was a marvelous fuck, though. I had never had a better fuck. It was the way she took it. She really digested a fuck. Her hands would grip me and her pussy clutched just as hard. Most fucks are really nothing, they are mostly labor, like trying to climb a very steep, muddy hill. But not Jan.

The phone rang. It rang several times before I could struggle out of bed and answer it.

"Mr. Chinaski?"

"Yes?"

"This is the Times Building."

"Yes?"

"We've reviewed your application and would like to employ you."

"Reporter?"

"No, maintenance man and janitor."

"All right."

"Report to Superintendent Barnes at the south door at 9 p.m."

"O.K."

I hung up. The phone had awakened Jan.

"Who was that?"

"I've got a job and I can't even walk. I report tonight. I don't know what the hell."

I moved back toward the bed like a sore-assed turtle and fell on it.

"We'll think of something."

"I can't wear clothes. I don't know what to do."

We stretched out, staring at the ceiling. Jan got up and went to the bathroom. When she came back she said, "I've got it!"

"Yeah!"

"I'll wrap you in gauze."

"Think it will work?"

"Sure."

Jan got dressed and went to the store. She came back with gauze, adhesive tape, and a bottle of muscatel. She got some ice cubes, made us each a drink and found some scissors. "O.K., let's do you up."

"Now wait, I don't have to be down there until 9 p.m. It's a night job."

"But I want to practice. Come on."

"All right. Shit."

"Put one knee up."

"All right. Easy."

"There, around and around we go. The old merry-go-round."

"Did anybody ever tell you how funny you are?"

"No."

"That's understandable."

"There. A little adhesive tape. A little bit more adhesive tape. There. Now lift the other knee, lover."

"Never mind the romance."

"Around and around and around. Your big fat legs."

"Your big fat ass."

"Now, now, now, be nice, lover. Some more adhesive tape. And a little bit more. You're good as new!"

"Like hell."

"Now for the balls, your big red balls. You are just in time for Christmas!"

"Wait! What are you going to do to my balls?"

"I'm going to wrap them."

"Isn't that dangerous? It might affect my tap dancing."

"It won't hurt anything."

"They'll slip out."

"I'll put them into a nice cocoon."

"Before you do, get me another drink."

I sat up with the drink and she began to wrap me.

"Around and around and around. Poor little balls. Poor big balls. What have they done to you? Around and around and around we go. Now for a little adhesive. And some more. And some more."

"Don't tape my balls to my asshole."

"Silly! I wouldn't do that! I love you!"

"Yeah."

"Now get up and walk around. Try walking around."

I got up and walked around the room slowly. "Hey, this feels all right! I feel like a eunuch but I feel all right."

"Maybe the eunuchs have it made."

"I do believe they have."

"How about a couple of soft boiled eggs?"

"Sure. I think I'm going to live."

Jan put a pot of water on the stove, dropped in four eggs, and we waited.

64

I WAS THERE at 9 p.m. The Superintendent showed me where the timeclock was. I punched in. He handed me three or four rags and a large jar. "There's a brass railing runs around this building. I want you to shine that brass railing." I walked outside and looked for the brass railing. It was there. It ran around the building. It was a large building. I put some polish on the railing and then rubbed it off with one of the rags. It didn't seem to do much good. People walked by and looked curiously at me. I'd had dull stupid jobs but this appeared to be the dullest and most stupid one of them all.

The idea, I decided, is not to think. But how do you stop thinking? Why was I chosen to polish this rail? Why couldn't I be inside writing editorials about municipal corruption? Well, it could be worse. I could be in China working a rice paddy.

I polished about twenty-five feet of the railing, turned the corner, and saw a bar across the street. I took my rags and jar across the street and went into the bar. There was nobody in there, just the bartender. "How ya doing?" he asked.

"Great. Give me a bottle of Schlitz."

He got one, opened it, took my money and rang it up.

"Where are the girls?" I asked.

"What girls?"

"You know. The girls."

"This is a nice place."

The door opened. It was Superintendent Barnes. "Can I buy you a beer?" I asked. He came over and stood beside me.

"Drink up, Chinaski, I'm giving you one last chance."

I drank the beer down and followed him out. We crossed the street together. "Evidently," he said, "you're not much good at polishing brass. Follow me." We went into the Times Building and up in an elevator together. We got out on one of the upper floors. "Now," he said, pointing to a long cardboard box on a desk, "that box contains fluorescent light tubes, new ones. You are to replace all burnt out light tubes. Take them out of the fixtures and put in the new ones. There's your ladder."

"O.K.," I said.

The Superintendent walked off and I was alone again. I was in some kind of storage loft. That room had the highest ceiling I had ever seen. The ladder stood thirty-six feet high. I had always had a fear of heights. I took a new light tube and slowly mounted the ladder. I had to remind myself again, try not to think. I climbed upwards. The fluorescent tubes were about five feet long. They broke easily and were hard to handle. When I reached the top of the ladder I peered down. That was a big mistake. A dizzy spell swept over me. I was a coward. I was up against a big window on one of the upper floors. I imagined myself falling off the ladder and out through the window, down through space until I hit the street. I watched the tiny automobiles cross back and forth down in the street below me, their headlights bright in the night. Then, very slowly, I reached up and removed a burnt out fluorescent light. I replaced it with a new light. Then I climbed down, feeling more relief with each step downward. When I reached the ground I promised myself that I'd never get on that ladder again.

I walked around reading things left on desks and tables. I walked into a glassed-off office. There was a note to somebody: "All right, we'll try this new cartoonist but he'd better be good. He'd better start good and stay good, we're not carrying anybody."

A door opened and there was Superintendent Barnes. "Chinaski, what are you doing in there?"

I came out of the office. "I'm a former student of journalism and I'm curious, sir."

"Is that all you've done? Replaced one light fixture?"

"Sir, I can't do it. I have a fear of heights."

"All right, Chinaski. I'm going to clock you out for tonight. You don't deserve another chance, but I want you to come back at 9 p.m. tomorrow night ready to do some work. And then we'll see."

"Yes, sir."

I walked with him toward the elevator. "Tell me," he asked, "how come you walk so funny?"

"I was frying some chicken in the pan and the grease exploded, it burned my legs."

"I thought maybe you had war wounds."

"No, the chicken did it."

We went down in the elevator together.

65

THE SUPERINTENDENT'S full name was Herman Barnes. Herman met me at the timeclock the next night and I punched in. "Follow me," he said. He took me into a very dimly lit room and introduced me to Jacob Christensen, who was to be my immediate supervisor. Barnes walked off.

Most of the people working at night in the Times Building were old, bent, defeated. They all walked around hunched over as if there was something wrong with their feet. We had all been assigned work overalls. "All right," said Jacob, "get your equipment." My equipment was a metal wagon, divided into two bins. In one half stood two mops, some rags and a large box of soap. The other half contained a variety of colored bottles and cans and boxes of supplies and more rags. It was evident that I was to be a janitor. Well, I had been a night janitor once before in San Francisco. You smuggled a bottle of wine in with you, worked like hell, and then when everybody else had gone, you sat looking out the windows, drinking wine and waiting for the dawn.

One of the old janitors came very close to me and screamed in my ear: *"These people are assholes, assholes! They have no intelligence! They don't know how to think! They're afraid of the mind! They're sick! They're cowards! They aren't thinking men like you and me!"*

His screams could be heard all over the room. He looked to be in his mid-sixties. The others were older, most of them looked seventy or more; about one third were women. They seemed used to the old fellow's antics. Nobody acted offended.

"They make me sick!" he screamed. *"No guts! Look at them! Hunks of shit!"*

"All right, Hugh," said Jacob, "take your stuff upstairs and get to work."

"I'll deck you, you bastard!" he screamed at the supervisor, *"I'll deck you right in your tracks!"*

"Get going, Hugh."

Hugh angrily rolled his wagon out of there, almost running down one of the old women.

"He's that way," Jacob said to me, "but he's the best janitor we've got."

"It's all right," I said, "I like an action place."

As I rolled my wagon along, Jacob told me my duties. I was responsible for two floors. The most important part was the restrooms. Restrooms were always first. Clean the sinks, the toilets, empty the baskets, get the mirrors, replace the handtowels, fill the soap containers, use lots and lots of deodorant, and be sure there's plenty of ass-wipe and paper toilet seat covers. And don't forget the sanitary napkins in the ladies' john! After that, get the wastebaskets in the offices and dust the desks. Then you take this machine here and wax the halls, and after you finish that . . .

"Yes, sir," I said.

The women's restrooms, as usual, were the worst. Many of the women, apparently, simply left their used sanitary napkins on the floor in the stalls, and the sight of them, although familiar, was disturbing, especially with a hangover. The men's restrooms were somewhat cleaner but then men didn't use sanitary napkins. At least I was alone when I worked. I wasn't too good a mopper; often a wad of hair or a crushed cigarette butt would remain conspicuously in one of the corners. I'd leave it there. I was conscientious with the ass-wipe and the paper seat covers, however: I could understand that. Nothing is worse than to finish a good shit, then reach over and find the toilet paper container empty. Even the most horrible human being on earth deserves to wipe his ass. Sometimes I have reached over and there's no paper and then when you reach for a toilet seat cover they're suddenly out of those too. You stand up and look down and yours has just fallen into the water. After that you have few alternatives. The one I find most satisfying is to wipe your ass with your shorts, dump them in there too, flush, and clog the toilet.

I finished both the ladies' and the men's restrooms, emptied the wastebaskets and dusted a few desks. Then I went back to the ladies crapper. They had sofas and chairs in there and an alarm clock. I had four hours left. I set the alarm to ring thirty minutes before quitting time. I stretched out on one of the couches and went to sleep.

The alarm wakened me. I stretched, splashed cold water on my face, and went down to the storage room with my gear. Old Hugh approached me. "Welcome to the land of the assholes," he said to me, more calmly this time. I didn't answer. It was dark in there and we only had ten minutes until punch-out time. We took off our overalls, and in most cases our street clothes were as dismal and as sad as our working clothes. We spoke very little or in whispers. I didn't mind the quiet. It was restful.

Then Hugh got right up next to my ear: "*Look at the jerks!*" he screamed, "*just look at the god damned jerks!*"

I walked away from him and stood at the other side of the room.

"*Are you one of them?*" he screamed across at me, "*are you an asshole too?*"

"Yes, noble sir."

"*How'd you like a foot up your ass?*" he screamed back.

"There's only empty space between us," I said.

Ancient warrior that he was, Hugh decided to close that space and he came in a hurry, leaping stiffly over a row of buckets. I stepped aside and he went flying past. He turned, came back grabbed me by the throat with both hands. He had long powerful fingers for such an old man; I could feel each one of them, even his thumbs. Hugh smelled like a sinkful of unwashed dishes. I tried to pry him loose but his grip only got stronger. Shots of red, blue and yellow flashed inside my head. I had no choice. I brought a knee up as gently as possible. I missed the first try, got him on the second. His fingers and thumbs loosened. Hugh fell to the floor, grabbing his parts. Jacob came up. "What happened here?"

"He called me an asshole, sir, and then he attacked me."

"Listen, Chinaski, this man is my best janitor. He's the best janitor I've had in fifteen years. Go easy on him, will you?" I walked over, got my time card and punched out. Peppery old Hugh looked up at me from the floor as I walked out: "I'm going to kill you, mister," he said.

Well, I thought, at least now he's polite. But that really didn't make me happy.

66

THE NEXT NIGHT I did about four hours work then went to the ladies' room, set the alarm and stretched out. I must have been asleep for about an hour when the door opened. It was Herman Barnes and Jacob Christensen. They looked at me; I raised my head and looked back, then put my head down on the cushion again. I heard them walk through into the crapper. When they came out I didn't look at them. I closed my eyes and pretended to be asleep.

The next day when I awakened about noon, I told Jan about it: "They caught me sleeping and didn't fire me. I guess I got them scared because of Hugh. It pays to be a tough son of a bitch. The world belongs to the strong."

"They're not going to let you get away with that."

"Balls. I've always told you I had it. I've got the touch. You might as well not have any god damned ears. You never listen to me."

"It's because you keep on saying the same thing over and over again."

"All right, let's have a drink and talk about it. You've been walking around with your ass up in the air since we got back together. Shit, I don't need you and you don't need me. Let's face up to the obvious."

Before the argument could start there was a knock on the door. "Hold it," I said and got into some pants. I opened the door and there was a Western Union delivery boy. I gave him a dime and opened the telegram:

HENRY CHINASKI: YOUR EMPLOYMENT WITH THE TIMES CO. HAS BEEN TERMIN-ATED.

HERMAN BARNES.

"What is it?" asked Jan.
"I've been canned."
"How about your check?"
"No mention."
"They owe you a check."
"I know. Let's go get it."
"O.K."

The car was gone. First it had lost its reverse gear, which was a challenge I overcame by continually planning ahead as we drove. Then the battery went dead which meant that the only way I could start it was coasting down a hill. I managed that for some weeks, then one night Jan and I got drunk and I forgot and parked it on a flat street outside a bar. It wouldn't start, of course, so I called an all-night garage and they came and towed it away. When I went to pick up the car a few days later they'd sunk $55 into repairing it and it still wouldn't start. I walked home and mailed them the pink slip.

So we had to walk to the Times Building. Jan knew I liked her in high heels so she put them on and we walked down there. It was a good twenty blocks one way. Jan sat down and rested on a bench outside and I walked up to the Payroll Department.

"I'm Henry Chinaski. I've been terminated and I'm here for my check."

"Henry Chinaski," said the girl, "wait a moment."

She looked through a sheaf of papers. "I'm sorry, Mr. Chinaski, but your check isn't ready yet."

"All right, I'll wait."

"We can't have your check ready until tomorrow, sir."

"But I've been terminated."

"I'm sorry. Tomorrow, sir."

I walked out. Jan got up from the bench. She looked hungry. "Let's hit the Grand Central Market for some stew meat and vegetables, then let's get a couple of bottles of good French wine."

"Jan, they said the check wasn't ready."

"But they have to give it to you. It's the law."

"I guess it is. I don't know. But they said the check would be ready tomorrow."

"Oh Christ, and I've walked all this way in high heels."

"You look good, baby."

"Yeah."

We started walking back. Halfway back Jan took off her heels and walked in her stocking feet. A couple of cars honked as we walked along. I gave each one of them the finger. When we got back there was enough money for tacos and beer. We got that, ate and drank, argued a bit, made love, and slept.

67

THE NEXT DAY about noon we started out again, Jan in her high heels. "I want you to make us some of that stew today," she said. "No man makes stew like you can. It's your greatest talent."

"Thanks a hell of a lot," I said.

It was still twenty blocks. Jan sat down on the bench

again and took off her shoes while I went to Payroll. It was the same girl.

"I'm Henry Chinaski," I said.

"Yes?"

"I was here yesterday."

"Yes?"

"You said my check would be ready today."

"Oh."

The girl went through her papers. "I'm sorry, Mr. Chinaski, but your check isn't here yet."

"But you said it would be ready."

"I'm sorry, sir, sometimes payroll checks take a little time to process."

"I want my check."

"I'm sorry, sir."

"You're not sorry. You don't know what sorrow is. I do. I want to see your boss's boss. Now."

The girl picked up a phone. "Mr. Handler? A Mr. Chinaski would like to see you about a termination payroll check."

There was some more small talk. Finally the girl looked at me. "Room 309."

I walked down to 309. The sign said "John Handler." I opened the door. Handler was alone. An officer and a director of the largest and most powerful newspaper in the West. I sat down in the chair across from him.

"Well, John," I said, "they booted my ass, caught me asleep in the ladies' crapper. Me and my old lady have walked down here two days running only to be told you don't have the check. Now, you know, that's pure crap. All I want to do is get that check and get drunk. That may not sound noble but it's my choice. If I don't get that check I'm not sure what I'll do."

Then I gave him a look straight out of "Casablanca."

"Got a smoke?"

John Handler gave me a smoke. He even lit it. Either they're going to throw a net over me or I'm going to get my check, I thought.

Handler picked up the phone. "Miss Simms. There's a check due a Mr. Henry Chinaski. I want it here within five minutes. Thank you." He hung up.

"Listen, John," I said, "I've had two years of journalism, L.A. City College. You couldn't use a reporter, could you?"

"Sorry, we're overstaffed now."

We chatted and after a few minutes a girl came in and handed John the check. He reached across the desk and handed it to me. A decent guy. I heard later that he died soon after that, but Jan and I got our beef stew and our vegetables and our French wine and we went on living.

68

I TOOK THE card they gave me at the State Department of Employment and walked over to the job interview. It was a few blocks east of Main Street and a little north of the skid row district. It was a company dealing with automobile brake parts. I showed them the card in the office and I filled out an application form. I lengthened my tenure at the jobs I had previously had, turning days into months and months into years. Most firms never bothered to check references. With those firms required to bond their employees, I didn't stand much chance. It would quickly appear that I had a police record. The brake supply house made no mention of a bond. Another problem after you had been on the job two or three weeks, most employers tried to get you to join their insurance plan, but by then I was usually gone.

The man glanced at my application and then turned humorously to the two women in the room: "This guy wants a job. Do you think he'll be able to stand us?"

Some jobs were amazingly easy to get. I remember one place I walked in, slouched down in a chair, and yawned. The guy behind the desk asked me: "Yes, what do you want?" "Oh hell," I answered, "I guess I need a job." "You're hired."

Some other jobs, however, were impossible for me to get. The Southern California Gas Company had ads in the help wanted section that promised high wages, early retirement, etc. I don't know how many times I went there and filled out their yellow application forms, how many times I sat on those hard chairs looking at large framed photos of pipes and gas storage tanks. I never came close to being hired and whenever I saw a gas man I would look at him very closely, trying to figure out what he had that I obviously didn't have.

The brake parts man took me up a narrow stairway. George Henley was his name. George showed me my workroom, very small, dark, just one lightbulb and one tiny window that looked out over an alley.

"Now," he said, "you see these cartons. You put the brake shoes into the cartons. Like this."

Mr. Henley showed me.

"We have three types of cartons, each printed differently. One carton is for our 'Super Durable Brake Shoe.' The other is for our 'Super Brake Shoe.' And the third is for our 'Standard Brake Shoe.' The brake shoes are stacked right here."

"But they all look alike to me. How can I tell them apart?"

"You don't. They're all the same. Just divide them into thirds. And when you finish packing all these shoes, come on downstairs and we'll find something else for you to do. O.K.?"

"O.K. When do I start?"

"You start now. And, absolutely no smoking. Not up here. If you have to smoke, you come on downstairs, O.K.?"

"O.K."

Mr. Henley closed the door. I heard him go down the stairs. I opened the little window and looked out at the world. Then I sat down, relaxed, and smoked a cigarette.

69

I QUICKLY LOST that job, just as I lost many others. But I didn't care—with one exception. It was the easiest job I ever had and I hated to see it go. It was during World War II. I was working for the Red Cross in San Francisco, driving a truck full of nurses and bottles and refrigerators around to various small towns. We collected blood for the war effort. I unloaded the trucks for the nurses when we arrived and then I had the rest of the day to walk around, sleep in the park, whatever. At the end of the day the nurses stuck the full bottles into the freezers and I squeezed blood clots out of the rubber tubes in the nearest crapper. I was usually sober but I pretended the blood clots were tiny fish or pretty little bugs which kept my lunch down.

The Red Cross job was a good one. I even had a date lined up with one of the nurses. But one morning I took the wrong bridge out of town and got lost in a skid row section somewhere with a truck full of nurses and needles and empty bottles. Those skid row guys were aching to rape the lot of us, and some of the nurses got nervous. It was back over the bridge for us and around some other way. I'd gotten my towns mixed up, and when we finally got to the church where the blood donors were waiting we were over two hours and fifteen minutes late. The front lawn was filled with angry donors and doctors and church officials. Across the Atlantic, Hitler was gaining with every step. I lost that job right then and there, unfortunately.

70

THE YELLOW CAB COMPANY in L.A. is located on the south side of Third Street. Rows and rows of yellow cabs sit in the sun in the yards. It is near the American Cancer Society. I had visited the American Cancer Society earlier, as I had understood it to be free. I had lumps all over my body, dizzy spells, I was spitting blood, and I had gone there only to be given an appointment for three weeks later. Now like every American boy I had always been told: *catch cancer early*. Then you go down to catch it early and they make you wait three weeks for an appointment. That's the difference between what we're told and actuality.

After three weeks I went back and they told me they could give me certain tests free, but that I could pass these tests and wouldn't really be sure that I didn't have cancer. However, if I gave them $25 and passed that test, I could be *fairly* sure I didn't have cancer. To be *absolutely* sure, after I had taken the $25 test, I would have to take the $75 test, and if I passed that one too, I could relax. It would mean my trouble was alcoholism or nerves or the clap. They talk real good and clear, those kittens in the white coats at the American Cancer Society, and I said, in other words, $100. Umm hum, they said, and I walked out and went on a three day toot and all the lumps vanished along with the dizzy spells and the blood spitting.

When I went to the Yellow Cab Company I passed the Cancer Building and I remembered that there were worse things than looking for a job you didn't want. I went in and it seemed easy enough, the same old forms, questions, etc. The only new thing was fingerprints but I knew how to be fingerprinted and I relaxed the hand and fingers and pressed them in the ink and the girl complimented me on my expertise. Mr. Yellow said to come back the next day to training class, and Jan and I celebrated that night.

71

JANEWAY SMITHSON WAS a little, insane, grey-haired bantam rooster of a man. He loaded five or six of us in one cab, and we rolled down to the bed of the L.A. River. Now in those days the L.A. River was a fake—there was no water, just a wide, flat, dry cement runway. The bums lived down there by the hundreds in little cement alcoves under the bridges and overpasses. Some of them even had potted plants in front of their places. All they needed to live like kings was canned heat (Sterno) and what they picked out of the nearby garbage dump. They were tan and relaxed and most of them looked a hell of a lot healthier than the average Los Angeles business man. Those guys down there had no problems with women, income tax, landlords, burial expenses, dentists, time payments, car repairs, or with climbing into a voting booth and pulling the curtain closed.

Janeway Smithson had been on the job for twenty-five years and was dumb enough to be proud of it. He carried a pistol in his right hip pocket and bragged that he had stopped a yellow cab in less time and fewer feet while taking the Brake Test than any other man in the history of the Yellow Cab Company. Looking at Janeway Smithson it occurred to me that this was either a lie or had been half-assed luck, and that Smithson, like any other twenty-five-year-man, was totally insane.

"O.K.," he said, "Bowers, you're first. Get this cock-sucker up to forty-five miles per hour and hold her there. I've got this gun in my right hand and a stopwatch in my left hand. When I fire, you hit the brakes. If you ain't got the reflexes to stop her quick enough, you'll be selling green bananas at noon at Seventh and Broadway ... No, you fucker! Don't watch my trigger finger! Look straight ahead! I'm going to sing you a little song. I'm going to lull you to sleep. You'll never guess when this son of a bitch is going to go off!"

It went off right then. Bowers hit the brakes. We lurched and skidded and spun. Clouds of dust billowed up from under the wheels as we whizzed between huge concrete pillars. Finally the cab screeched to a stop and rocked back and forth. Somebody in the back seat got a nosebleed.

"Did I make it?" Bowers asked.

"I ain't gonna tell you," said Smithson, making a notation in his little black book. "O.K., De Esprito, you're next."

De Esprito took the wheel and we went through more of the same. The drivers kept changing as we ran up and down the L.A. riverbed, burning brakes and rubber and shooting off the pistol. I was last to try it. "Chinaski," said Smithson.

I took the wheel and ran the cab up to fifty m.p.h.

"You set the record, eh Pops? I'm going to shoot your ass right off the map!"

"What?"

"Blow out the earwax! I'm going to take you, Pops! I once shook hands with Max Baer! I was once a gardener for Tex Ritter! Kiss your ass goodbye!"

"You're *ridin'* the god damned brake! Take your foot off the god damned brake!"

"Sing me a song, Pops! Sing me your little song! I've got forty love letters from Mae West in my dufflebag!"

"You can't beat me!"

I didn't wait for the gun. I hit the brakes. I guessed right. The gun and my foot hit at the same time. I beat his world record by fifteen feet and nine-tenths of a second. That's what he said at first. Then he changed his tune and said that I had cheated. I said, "O.K., write me up for whatever you want, but just get us out of the L.A. River. It's not going to rain so we won't be able to catch any fish."

72

THERE WERE FORTY or fifty of us in the Training Class. We all sat at little desks, rows of them bolted to the floor. Each desk had a flat area like an arm rest to the right hand side. It was just like the old days in a biology or chemistry class.

Smithson called roll.

"Peters!"

"Yep."

"Calloway."

"Uh huh."

"McBride . . ."

(Silence).

"McBride?"

"Oh, ya."

The roll call continued. I thought it was very nice that there were so many job openings, yet it worried me too—we'd probably be pitted against one another in some way. Survival of the fittest. There were always men looking for jobs in America. There were always all these usable bodies. And I wanted to be a writer. Almost everybody was a writer. Not everybody thought they could be a dentist or an automobile mechanic but everybody knew they could be a writer. Of those fifty guys in the room, probably fifteen of them thought they were writers. Almost everybody used words and could write them down, i.e., almost everybody could be a writer. But most men, fortunately, aren't writers, or even cab drivers, and some men—many men—unfortunately aren't anything.

The roll call was over. Smithson looked around the room. "We are gathered here," he began, then stopped. He looked at a black man in the first row. "Spencer?"

"Yes."

"You took the wire out of your cap, didn't you?"

"Yes."

"Now you see, you'll be sitting in your cab with your cap down over your ears like Doug McArthur and some old woman with a shopping bag will walk up and want to take a cab and you'll be sitting there like that with your arm hanging out the window and she'll think you're a cowboy. She'll think you're a cowboy and she won't ride with you. She'll take a bus. That stuff is all right in the army, but this is *Yellow Cab*."

Spencer reached down on the floor, got the wire and put it back in his cap. He needed the job.

"Now most guys think they know how to drive. But the fact is very few people know how to drive, they just steer. Everytime I drive down the street I marvel at the fact that there isn't an accident every few seconds. Every day I see two or three people simply run through red lights as if they didn't exist. I'm no preacher but I can tell you this—the lives that people lead are driving them crazy and their insanity comes out in the way they drive. I'm not here to tell you how to live. You'll have to see your rabbi or your priest or your local whore. I'm here to teach you how to drive. I'm trying to keep our insurance rates down, and to fix it so you can get back to your room alive at night."

"God damn," said the kid next to me, "old Smithson's something, ain't he?"

"Every man is a poet," I said.

"Now," said Smithson, "and, god damn you, McBride, wake up and listen to me . . . now, when is the only time a man can lose control of his cab and won't be able to help it?"

"When I get a hard-on?" said some cracker.

"Mendoza, if you can't drive with a hard-on we can't use you. Some of our best men drive with hard-ons all day long and all night too."

The boys laughed.

"Come on, when is the only time a man can lose control of his cab and won't be able to help it?" Nobody answered. I raised my hand.

"Yes, Chinaski?"

"A man might lose control of his cab when he sneezed."

"That's correct."

I felt like a star pupil again. It was like the old L.A. City College days—bad grades, but good with the mouth.

"All right, when you sneeze, what do you do?"

As I raised my hand again the door opened and a man entered the room. He walked down the aisle and stood before me. "Are you Henry Chinaski?"

"Yes."

He snatched my cabbie's cap from my head, almost angrily. Everybody looked at me. Smithson's face was expressionless and impartial.

"Follow me," said the man.

I followed him out of the study hall and into his office.

"Sit down."

I sat down.

"We ran a check on you, Chinaski."

"Yes?"

"You have eighteen common drunks and one drunk driving."

"I thought if I put it down I wouldn't get hired."

"You lied to us."

"I've stopped drinking."

"It doesn't matter. Once you've falsified your application, you're disqualified."

I got up and walked out. I walked down the sidewalk past the Cancer Building. I walked back to our apartment. Jan was in bed. She was wearing a torn pink slip. One shoulder strap was held together by a safety pin. She was already drunk. "How'd you make out, daddy?"

"They don't want me."

"How come?"

"They don't want homosexuals."

"Oh, well. There's wine in the fridge. Get yourself a glass and come on to bed."

That I did.

73

A COUPLE OF days later I found an ad in the paper for a shipping clerk in an art supply store. The store was very close to where we lived but I overslept and it wasn't until 3 p.m. that I got down there. The manager was talking to an applicant when I arrived. I didn't know how many others he had interviewed. A girl gave me a form to fill out. The guy seemed to be making a good impression on the manager. They were both laughing. I filled out the form and waited. Finally the manager called me over.

"I want to tell you something. I already accepted another job this morning," I told him. "Then I happened to see your ad. I live right around the corner. I thought it might be nicer to work so close to home. Besides, I paint as a hobby. I thought I might get a discount on some of the art supplies I need."

"We give 15% off to employees. What is the name of this other place that hired you?"

"Jones-Hammer Arc Light Company. I'm to supervise their shipping department. They're on lower Alameda Street just below the slaughterhouse. I'm supposed to report at 8 a.m."

"Well, we still want to interview some more applicants."

"It's all right. I didn't expect to take this job. I just dropped in because it was nearby. You have my phone number on the application. But once I go to work at Jones-Hammer, it wouldn't be fair for me to leave them."

"You're married?"

"Yes. With one child. A boy. Tommy, age 3."

"All right. We'll let you know."

THE PHONE rang at 6:30 p.m. that evening. "Mr. Chinaski?"

"Yes?"

"Do you still want the job?"

"Where?"

"At the Graphic Cherub Art Supply."

"Well, yes."

"Then report at 8:30 a.m."

74

BUSINESS DIDN'T SEEM to be too good. Outgoing orders were few and small. The manager, Bud, walked back to where I was leaning against the shipping table smoking a cigar. "When things are slow you can go get yourself a cup of coffee at the cafe around the corner. But be sure you're back here when the trucks come by for the pickups."

"Sure."

"And keep your squeegie rack filled. Keep a good supply of squeegies."

"All right."

"Also keep your eyes peeled and see that nobody comes in from the back and steals our stock. We got a lotta winos roaming these alleys."

"O.K."

"You got plenty of FRAGILE labels?"

"Yes."

"Don't be afraid to use plenty of FRAGILE labels. If you run out, let me know. Pack the stuff good, especially the paints in glass."

"I'll take care of everything."

"O.K. And when things get slow you walk down the alley and get yourself a cup of coffee. It's Montie's Cafe. They got a waitress there with big tits, you ought to see them. She wears low-cut blouses and bends over all the time. And the pie is fresh."

"O.K."

75

MARY LOU WAS one of the girls in the front office. Mary Lou had style. She drove a three year old Cadillac and lived with her mother. She entertained members of the L.A. Philharmonic, movie directors, cameramen, lawyers, real estate agents, chiropractors, holy men, ex-aviators, ballet dancers and other entertainment figures such as wrestlers and defensive left ends. But she had never married and she had never gotten out of the front office of Graphic Cherub Art Supply, except now and then for a quickie fuck with Bud in the ladies' room, giggling, with the door bolted after she thought the rest of us had gone home. Also, she was religious and loved to play the horses, but preferably from a reserved seat and preferably at Santa Anita. She looked down on Hollywood Park. She was desperate and she was choosey at the same time and, in a way, beautiful, but she didn't have quite enough going for her to become what she imagined herself to be.

One of her jobs was to bring a copy of the orders back to me after she had typed them. The clerks picked up another copy of the same orders out of the basket to fill when they weren't waiting on customers, and I'd match them up before I packed the stuff. The first time she came back with some orders she wore a tight black skirt, high heels, a white blouse, and a gold and black scarf around her neck. She had a cute turned-up nose, a marvelous behind and fine breasts. She was tall. Class.

"Bud tells me you paint," she said.

"A bit."

"Oh, I think that's marvelous. We have such interesting people working here."

"What do you mean?"

"Well, we have a janitor, an old man, Maurice, he's from France. He comes once a week and cleans the store. He paints too. He buys all his paints and brushes and canvas from us. But he's strange. He never speaks, just nods and points. He just points to things he wants to buy."

"Uh huh."

"He's strange."

"Uh huh."

"Last week I went into the ladies' room, and he was there, mopping up in the dark. He'd been in there an hour."

"Uh."

"You don't talk either."

"Oh yes. I'm all right."

Mary Lou turned and walked away. I watched the buttocks work on that tall body. Magic. Some women were magic.

I had packed a few orders when this old guy came

walking down the aisle. He had a grubby grey mustache that drooped around his mouth. He was small and bent. He was dressed in black, had a red scarf tied around his throat, and he word a blue beret. Out from under the blue beret came much long grey hair, uncombed.

Maurice's eyes were the most distinctive thing about him; they were a vivid green and seemed to look out from deep within his head. He had bushy eyebrows. He was smoking a long thin cigar. "Hi, kid," he said. Maurice didn't have much of a French accent. He sat on the end of the packing table and crossed his legs.

"I thought you didn't talk?"

"Oh, that. Balls. I wouldn't piss on a fly for them. Why bother?"

"How come you clean the crapper in the dark?"

"That's Mary Lou. I look at her. Then I go in there and come all over the floor. I mop it up. She knows."

"You paint?"

"Yes, I'm working on a canvas in my room now. As big as this wall. Not a mural. A canvas. I am painting a man's life—from his birth through the vagina, through all the years of his existence, then finally into the grave. I look at people in the park. I use them. That Mary Lou, she'd make one good fuck, what?"

"Maybe. It could be a mirage."

"I lived in France. I met Picasso."

"Did you really?"

"Shit, I did. He's O.K."

"How'd you meet him?"

"I knocked on his door."

"Was he pissed?"

"No. No, he wasn't pissed."

"Some people don't like him."

"Some people don't like anybody who is famous."

"And some people don't like anybody who isn't."

"People don't count. I wouldn't piss on a fly for them."

"What'd Picasso say?"

"Well, I asked him. I said, 'Master, what can I do to make my work better?'"

"No shit?"

"No shit."

"What'd he say?"

"He said, 'I can't tell you anything about your work. You must do it all by yourself.'"

"Ha."

"Yes."

"Pretty good."

"Yes. Got a match?"

I gave him some. His cigar had gone out.

"My brother is rich," said Maurice. "He has disowned me. He doesn't like my drinking. He doesn't like my painting."

"But your brother never met Picasso."

Maurice stood up and smiled.

"No, he never met Picasso."

Maurice walked back down the aisle toward the front of the store, cigar smoke curling back over his shoulder. He had kept my book of matches.

76

BUD CAME BACK pushing three one gallon cans of paint on the order wagon. He put them on the packing table. They were labeled *crimson*. He handed me three labels. The labels said *vermillion*.

"We're out of vermillion," he said. "Soak off these labels and paste on the *vermillion* labels."

"There's quite a difference between crimson and vermillion," I said.

"Just do it."

Bud left me some rags and a razor blade. I soaked the rags in water and wrapped them around the cans. Then I scraped off the old labels and glued on the new ones.

He came back a few minutes later. He had a can of *ultramarine* and a label for *cobalt blue*. Well, he was getting closer . . .

77

PAUL WAS ONE of the clerks. He was fat, about 28. His eyes were very large, bulging. He was on pills. He showed me a handful. They were all different sizes and colors.

"Want some?"

"No."

"Go ahead. Take one."

"All right."

I took a yellow.

"I take 'em all," he said. "Damn things. Some want to take me up, some want to take me down. I let them fight over me."

"That's supposed to be rough on you."

"I know. Say, why don't you come to my place after work?"

"I've got a woman."

"We've all got women. I've got something better."

"What?"

"My girlfriend bought me this reducing machine for my birthday. We fuck on it. It moves up and down, we don't have to do any work. The machine does all the work."

"It sounds good."

"You and I can use that machine. It makes a lot of noise but as long as we don't use it after 10 p.m. it's O.K."

"Who gets on top?"

"What difference does it make? I can take it or give it. Top or bottom, it doesn't matter."

"Doesn't it?"

"Hell no. We'll flip for it."

"Let me think it over."

"All right. Want another pill?"

"Yeah. Give me another yellow."

"I'll check with you at closing time."

"Sure."

PAUL WAS there at closing.

"Well?"

"I can't do it, Paul. I'm straight."

"It's a great machine. Once you get on that machine you'll forget everything."

"I can't do it."

"Well, come on over and look at my pills anyhow."

"All right. I can do that."

I locked the back door. Then we walked out the front together. Mary Lou was sitting in the office smoking a cigarette and talking to Bud.

"Good night, men," said Bud with a big grin on his face . . .

PAUL'S PLACE was a block off to the south. He had a lower front apartment with the windows facing Seventh Street.

"There's the machine," he said. He turned it on.

"Look at it, look at it. It sounds like a washing machine. The woman upstairs, she sees me in the hall and she says, 'Paul you must really be a clean guy. I hear you washing your clothes three or four times a week.'"

"Turn it off," I said.

"Look at my pills. I've got thousands of pills, *thousands*. I don't even know what some of them are."

Paul had all the bottles on the coffee table. There were

eleven or twelve bottles, all different sizes and shapes and filled with colored pills. They were beautiful. As I watched he opened a bottle and took three or four pills out of it and swallowed them. Then he opened another bottle and took a couple of pills. Then he opened a third bottle.

"Come on, what the hell," he said. "let's get on the machine."

"I'll take a rain check. I got to go."

"All right," he said, "if you won't fuck me, I'll fuck myself!"

I closed the door behind me and walked out on the street. I heard him turn on the machine.

78

MR. MANDERS WALKED back to where I was working and stood and looked at me. I was packing a large order of paints and he stood there watching me. Manders had been the original owner of the store but his wife had run off with a black man and he had started drinking. He drank his way out of the ownership. Now he was just a salesman and another man owned his store.

"You putting FRAGILE labels on these cartons?"

"Yes."

"Do you pack them well? Plenty of newspaper and straw?"

"I think I'm doing it right."

"Do you have enough FRAGILE labels?"

"Yes, there's a whole boxfull under the bench here."

"Are you sure you know what you're doing? You don't look like a shipping clerk."

"What does a shipping clerk look like?"

"They wear aprons. You don't wear an apron."

"Oh."

"Smith-Barnsley called to say that they had received a broken pint jar of rubber cement in a shipment."

I didn't answer.

"You let me know if you run out of FRAGILE labels."

"Sure."

Manders walked off down the aisle. Then he stopped and turned and watched me. I ripped some tape off the dispenser and with an extra flourish I wrapped it around the carton. Manders turned and walked away.

BUD CAME running back. "How many six-foot squeegies you got in stock?"

"None."

"This guy wants five six-foot squeegies now. He's waiting for them. Make them up."

Bud ran off. A squeegie is a piece of board with a rubber edge. It's used in silk-screening. I went to the attic, got the lumber down, measured off five six-foot sections, and sawed the boards. Then I began drilling holes into the wood along one edge. You bolted the rubber into place after drilling the holes. Then you had to sand the rubber down until it was level, a perfectly straight edge. If the rubber edge wasn't perfectly straight, the silk-screen process wouldn't work. And the rubber had a way of curling and warping and resisting.

Bud was back in three minutes. "You got those squeegies ready yet?"

"No."

He ran back to the front. I drilled, turned screws, sanded. In five more minutes he was back. "You got those squeegies ready yet?"

"No."

He ran off.

I had one six-foot squeegie finished and was halfway through another when he came back again.

"Never mind. He left."
Bud walked back up toward the front . . .

79

THE STORE WAS going broke. Each day the orders were smaller and smaller. There was less and less to do. They fired Picasso's buddy and had me mop the crappers, empty the baskets, hang the toilet paper. Each morning I swept and watered the sidewalk in front of the store. Once a week I washed the windows.

One day I decided to clean up my own quarters. One of the things I did was to clean out the carton area where I kept all the empty cartons I used for shipping. I got them all out of there and swept up the trash. As I was cleaning up I noticed a small oblong grey box at the bottom of the bin. I picked it up and opened it. It contained twenty-four large-sized camel hair brushes. They were fat and beautiful and sold for $10 each. I didn't know what to do. I looked at them for some time, then closed the lid, walked out the back and put them in a trashcan in the alley. Then I put all the empty cartons back in the bin.

That night I left as late as possible. I walked to the nearby cafe and had a coffee and apple pie. Then I came out, walked down the block, and turned up the alley. I walked up the alley and was a quarter of the way when I saw Bud and Mary Lou enter the alley from the other end. There was nothing to do but to keep walking. It was final. We got closer and closer. Finally as I passed them I said, "Hi." They said, "Hi." I kept walking. I walked out the other end of the alley and across the street and into a bar. I sat down. I sat there and had a beer and then had another. A woman down the bar asked me if I had a match. I got up and lighted her cigarette; as I did that, she farted. I asked her if she lived in the neighborhood. She said she was from Montana. I remembered an unhappy night I'd had in Cheyenne, Wyoming, which is near Montana. Finally I left and walked back to the alley.

I went up to the trashcan and reached in. It was still there: the oblong grey box. It didn't feel empty. I slipped it through the neck of my shirt and it dropped down, slipped down, slid down against my gut and lay there. I walked back to where I lived.

80

THE NEXT THING that happened was that they hired a Japanese girl. I had always had a very strange idea, for a long time, that after all the trouble and pain was over, that a Japanese girl would come along one day and we would live happily ever after. Not so much happily, as *easily* and with deep understanding and mutual concern. Japanese women had a beautiful bone structure. The shape of the skull, and the tightening of the skin with age, was a lovely thing; the skin of the drum drawn taut. With American women the face got looser and looser and finally fell apart. Even their bottoms fell apart and became indecent. The strength of the two cultures was very different too: Japanese women instinctively understood yesterday and today and tomorrow. Call it wisdom. And they had staying power. American women only knew today and tended to come to pieces when just one day went wrong.

So I was very taken with the new girl. Also I was still drinking heavily with Jan which befuddled the brain, gave it a strange airy feeling, made it take strange twists and turns, gave it courage. So the first day she came back with the orders I said, "Hey, let's touch. I want to kiss you."

"What?"

"You heard me."

She walked away. As she did I noticed she had a slight limp. It figured: the pain and the weight of centuries . . .

I kept after her like a horny redneck drunk on beer in a Greyhound bus passing through Texas. She was intrigued—she understood my craziness. I was enchanting her without realizing it.

One day a customer telephoned to ask if we had gallon cans of white glue in stock and she came back to check some cartons stacked in one corner. I saw her and asked if I might help. She said, "I'm looking for a carton of glue stamped 2-G."

"2-G," I said, "huh?"

I put my arm around her waist.

"We're going to make it. You are the wisdom of centuries and I am me. We are meant for each other."

She began to giggle like an American woman. "Japanese girls don't do that. What the hell's the matter with you?"

She rested against me. I noticed a row of paint cartons pushed against the wall. I led her over and gently sat her on the row of cartons. I pushed her down. I climbed on top of her and began kissing her, pulling up her dress. Then Danny, one of the clerks walked in. Danny was a virgin. Danny went to painting class at night and fell asleep during the day. He couldn't separate art from cigarette butts. "What the hell's going on here?" he asked, and then he walked swiftly away toward the front office.

Bud called me into the front office the next day. "You know, we had to let her go too."

"It wasn't her fault."

"She was with you back there."

"I instigated."

"She submitted, according to Danny."

"What does Danny know about submission? The only thing he has ever submitted to is his hand."

145

"He saw you."

"Saw what? I didn't even have her panties off."

"This is a business house."

"There's Mary Lou."

"I hired you because I thought you were a dependable shipping clerk."

"Thanks. And I end up getting fired for trying to fuck a slant-eyed squaw with a gimp in her left leg on top of forty gallons of auto paint—which, by the way, you've been selling to the L.A. City College Art Department as the real thing. I ought to turn you over to the Better Business Bureau."

"Here's your check. You're finished."

"All right. See you at Santa Anita."

"Sure," he said.

There was an extra day's pay on the check. We shook hands and I walked out.

81

THE NEXT JOB didn't last long either. It was little more than a stopover. It was a small company specializing in Christmas items: lights, wreaths, Santa Clauses, paper trees, all that. When I was hired they told me that they'd have to let me go the day before Thanksgiving; that there wasn't any business after Thanksgiving. There were a half-dozen of us hired under the same conditions. They called us "warehousemen" and mainly we loaded and unloaded trucks. Also, a warehouseman is a guy who stands around a lot smoking cigarettes, in a dream-like state. But we didn't last until Thanksgiving, the half-dozen of us. It was my idea that we go to a bar everyday for lunch. Our lunch periods became longer and longer. One afternoon we simply didn't return. But the next morning, like good guys, we were all there. We were told we were no longer wanted. "Now," said the manager, "I've got to hire a whole new god damned crew." "And fire them on Thanksgiving," said one of us. "Listen," said the manager, "you guys want to work one more day?" "So you'll have time to interview and hire our replacements?" asked one of us. "Take it or leave it," said the manager. We took it and we worked all day, laughing like hell, throwing cartons through the air. Then we picked up our final checks and went back to our rooms and our drunken women.

82

IT WAS ANOTHER fluorescent light fixture house: The Honeybeam Company. Most of the cartons were five or six feet long, and heavy when packed. We worked a ten hour day. The procedure was quite simple—you went out to the assembly line and got your parts, brought them back, and packed them up. Most of the workers were Mexican and black. The blacks worked on me and accused me of having a smart mouth. The Mexicans stood back quietly and watched. Each day was a battle—both for my life and my ability to keep up with the lead packer, Monty. They worked on me all day long.

"Hey, boy. Boy! Come 'ere, boy! Boy, I want to talk to you!"

It was little Eddie. Little Eddie was good at it.

I didn't answer.

"Boy, I'm talking to you!"

"Eddie, how'd you like to have a jack-handle slid up your ass while you're singing 'Old Man River'?"

"How'd you get all those holes in your face, white boy? Fall on a drill while you were asleep?"

"Where'd you get that scar on your lower lip? Your boyfriend keep his razor strapped to his dick?"

I went out at breaktime and traded a few with Big Angel. Big Angel whipped me but I got in some shots, didn't panic, and held my ground. I knew he had only ten minutes to work on me and that helped. What hurt most was a thumb he got in my eye. We walked back in together, huffing and puffing.

"You're no pro," he said.

"Try me sometime when I'm not hungover. I'll run you right off the lot."

"O.K.," he said, "come in some time sweet and clean and we'll try it again."

I decided right then to never come in sweet and clean.

MORRIS WAS the foreman. He had terribly flat vibes. It was as if he were made of wood, clear through. I tried not to talk to him more than I had to. He was the son of the owner and had tried to make it as a salesman, outside. He failed and they brought him back inside. He walked up. "What happened to your *eye*? It's all *red*."

"I was walking under a palm tree and I was attacked by a blackbird."

"He got your eye?"

"He got it."

Morris walked off, the crotch of his pants was jammed up into his ass . . .

THE BEST part was when the assembly line couldn't keep up with us and we stood around waiting. The assembly line was manned mostly by young Mexican girls with beautiful skin and dark eyes; they wore tight bluejeans and tight sweaters and gaudy earrings. They were so young and healthy and efficient and relaxed. They were good workers, and now and then one would look up and say something and then there would be explosions of laughter and glances as I watched them laugh in their tight bluejeans and their tight sweaters and thought, if one of them was in bed with me tonight I could take all this shit a whole lot better. We all were thinking that. And we were also thinking, they all belong to somebody else. Well, what the hell. It didn't make any difference. In fifteen years they'd weigh 185 pounds and it would be their daughters who were beautiful.

I bought an eight-year-old automobile and stayed on the job there through December. Then came the Christmas party. That was December 24th. There were to be drinks, food, music, dancing. I didn't like parties. I didn't know how to dance and people frightened me, especially people at parties. They attempted to be sexy and gay and witty and although they hoped they were good at it, they weren't. They were bad at it. Their trying so hard only made it worse.

So when Jan leaned up against me and said, "Fuck that party, stay home with me. We'll get drunk here," I didn't find that very hard to do.

I heard about the party the day after Christmas. Little Eddie said, "Christine cried when you didn't show up."

"Who?"

"Christine, the cute little Mexican girl."

"Who's that?"

"She works on the back row, in assembly."

"Cut the shit."

"Yeah. She cried and cried. Somebody drew a great big picture of you with your goatee and hung it on the wall and underneath they wrote, 'Give me another drink!'"

"I'm sorry, man. I got tied up."

"It's all right. She finally stopped being mad and danced with me. She got drunk and threw up some cake and she got drunker and danced with all the black guys. She dances real sexy. She finally went home with Big Angel."

"Big Angel probably stuck his thumb in her eye," I said.

* * *

149

THE DAY before New Year's after the afternoon break, Morris called me over and said, "I want to talk to you."

"O.K."

"Over here."

Morris walked me over to a dark corner next to a row of stacked packing boxes. "Listen, we're going to have to let you go."

"All right. This is my last day?"

"Yes."

"Will the check be ready?"

"No, we'll mail it."

"All right."

83

NATIONAL BAKERY GOODS was located nearby. They gave me a white smock and a locker. They made cookies, biscuits, cupcakes and so forth. Because I had claimed two years of college on my application, I got the job as Coconut Man. The Coconut Man stood up on a perch, scooped his shovel into the shredded coconut barrel and dumped the white flakes into a machine. The machine did the rest: it spit coconut on the cakes and other sundry items passing below. It was an easy job and a dignified one. There I was, dressed in white, scooping white shredded coconut into a machine. On the other side of the room were dozens of young girls, also dressed in white, with white caps on. I wasn't quite sure what they were doing but they were busy. We worked nights.

It happened my second night. It began slowly, a couple of the girls began singing, "Oh, Henry, oh Henry, how you can love! Oh, Henry, oh Henry, heaven's above!" More and more girls joined in. Soon they were all singing. I thought, surely, they were singing to me.

The girls' supervisor rushed up screaming, "*All right, all right, girls, that's enough!*"

I dipped my shovel calmly into the shredded coconut and accepted it all . . .

I HAD been there two or three weeks when a bell rang during the late shift. A voice came over the intercom. "All the men come to the rear of the building."

A man in a business suit walked toward us. "Gather around me," he said. He had a clipboard with a sheet of paper on it. The men circled him. We were all dressed in white smocks. I stood at the edge of the circle.

"We are entering our slack period," said the man. "I'm sorry to say that we're going to have to let all of you go until things pick up. Now, if you'll line up in front of me, I'll take your names, phone numbers and addresses. When things get better, you'll be the first to know."

The men began to form a line but with much jostling and cursing. I didn't get into line. I looked at all my fellow workers dutifully giving their names and addresses. These, I thought, are the men who dance beautifully at parties. I walked back to my locker, hung up the white smock, left my shovel leaning against the door, and walked out.

84

THE HOTEL SANS was the best in the city of Los Angeles. It was an old hotel but it had class and a charm missing from the newer places. It was directly across from the park downtown.

It was renowned for businessmens' conventions and expensive hookers of almost legendary talent—who at the end of a lucrative evening had even been known to give the bellboys a little. There also were stories of bellboys who had become millionaires—bloody bellboys with eleven inch dicks who had had the good fortune to meet and marry some rich, elderly guest. And the *food*, the LOBSTER, the huge black chefs in very tall white hats who knew everything, not only about food but about Life and about me and about everything.

I was assigned to the loading dock. That loading dock had *style*: for each truck that came in there were ten guys to unload it when it only took two at the most. I wore my best clothes. I never touched anything.

We unloaded (they unloaded) everything that came into the hotel and most of it was foodstuffs. My guess was that the rich ate more lobster than anything else. Crates and crates of them would come in, deliciously pink and large, waving their claws and feelers.

"You like those things, don't you, Chinaski?"

"Yeah. Oh yeah," I'd drool.

One day the lady in the employment office called me over. The employment office was at the rear of the loading dock. "I want you to manage this office on Sundays, Chinaski." "What do I do?" "Just answer the phone and hire the Sunday dishwashers." "All right!"

THE FIRST Sunday was nice. I just sat there. Soon an old guy walked in. "Yeah, buddy?" I asked. He had on an expensive suit, but it was wrinkled and a little dirty; and the cuffs were just starting to go. He was holding his hat in his hand. "Listen," he asked, "do you need somebody who is a good conversationalist? Somebody who can meet and talk to people? I have a certain amount of charm, I tell gracious stories, I can make people laugh."

"Yeah?"

"Oh, yes."

"Make me laugh."

"Oh, you don't understand. The setting has to be right, the mood, the *decor*, you know . . ."

"Make me laugh."

"Sir . . ."

"Can't use you, you're a stiff!"

THE DISHWASHERS were hired at noon. I stepped out of the office. Forty bums stood there. "All right now, we need five good men! Five *good* ones! No winos, perverts, communists, or child-molesters! And you've got to have a social security card! All right now, get them out and hold them up in the air!"

Out came the cards. They waved them.

"Hey, I got one!"

"Hey, buddy, over here! Give a guy a break!"

I slowly looked them over. "O.K., you with the shit-stain on your collar," I pointed. "Step forward."

"That's no shit stain, sir. That's gravy."

"Well, I don't know, buddy, looks to me like you been eatin' more crotch than roast beef!"

"Ah, hahaha," went the bums, "Ah, hahaha!"

"O.K., now, I need *four* good dishwashers! I have four pennies here in my hand. I'm going to toss them up. The four men who bring me back a penny get to wash dishes today!"

I tossed the pennies high into the air above the crowd. Bodies jumped and fell, clothing ripped, there were curses, one man screamed, there were several fistfights. Then the lucky four came forward, one at a time, breathing heavily, each with a penny. I gave them their work cards and waved them toward the employees' cafeteria where they would first be fed. The other bums retreated slowly down the loading ramp, jumped off, and walked down the alley into the wasteland of downtown Los Angeles on a Sunday.

85

SUNDAYS WERE BEST because I was alone and soon I began to take a pint of whiskey to work with me. One Sunday after a hard night's drinking the bottle got to me; I blacked-out. I vaguely remembered some unusual activity that evening after I went home but it was unclear. I told Jan about it the next morning before I went back to work. "I think I fucked up. But maybe it's my imagination."

I went in and walked up to the timeclock. My timecard was not in the rack. I turned and walked over to the old lady who ran the employment office. When she saw me she looked nervous. "Mrs. Farrington, my timecard is missing."

"Henry, I always thought you were such a nice boy."

"Yes?"

"You don't remember what you did, do you?" she asked, looking nervously around.

"No, Ma'am."

"You were drunk. You cornered Mr. Pelvington in the men's locker room and you wouldn't let him out. You held him captive for thirty minutes."

"What did I do to him?"

"You wouldn't let him out."

"Who is he?"

"The Assistant Manager of this hotel."

"What else did I do?"

"You were lecturing him on how to run this hotel. Mr. Pelvington has been in the hotel business for thirty years. You suggested that prostitutes be registered on the first floor only and that they should be given regular physical examinations. There are no prostitutes in this hotel, Mr. Chinaski."

"Oh, I know that, Mrs. Pelvington."

"Farrington."

"Mrs. Farrington."

"You also told Mr. Pelvington that only two men were needed on the loading dock instead of ten, and that it would cut down on the theft if each employee was given one live lobster to take home each night in a specially constructed cage that could be carried on buses and streetcars."

"You have a real sense of humor, Mrs. Farrington."

"The security guard couldn't get you to let go of Mr. Pelvington. You tore his coat. It was only after we called the regular police that you relented."

"I presume I'm terminated?"

"You have presumed correctly, Mr. Chinaski."

I walked off behind a stack of crates. When Mrs. Farrington wasn't looking I cut for the employees' cafeteria. I still had my food card. I could get one last good meal. The stuff was nearly as good as what they cooked for the guests upstairs, plus they gave the help more of it. Clutching my food card I walked into the cafeteria, picked up a tray, a knife and fork, a cup and some paper napkins. I walked up to the food counter. Then I looked up. Tacked to the wall behind the counter was a piece of white cardboard covered with a large crude scrawl:

DON'T GIVE ANY FOOD TO HENRY CHINASKI

I put the tray back unnoticed. I walked out of the cafeteria. I walked along the loading dock, then I jumped into the alley. Coming toward me was another bum. "Got a smoke, buddy?" he asked. "Yeah." I took out two, gave him one, took one myself. I lit him up, then I lit myself up. He moved east and I moved west.

86

THE FARM LABOR MARKET was at Fifth and San Pedro Streets. You reported at 5 a.m. It was still dark when I got there. Men were sitting and standing around, rolling cigarettes and talking quietly. All such places always have the same smell—the smell of stale sweat, urine, and cheap wine.

The day before I had helped Jan move in with a fat real estate operator who lived on Kingsley Drive. I'd stood back out of sight in the hall and watched him kiss her; then they'd gone into his apartment together and the door had closed. I had walked back down the street alone noticing for the first time the pieces of blown paper and accumulated trash that littered the street. We'd been evicted from our apartment. I had $2.08. Jan promised me she'd be waiting when my luck changed but I hardly believed that. The real estate operator's name was Jim Bemis, he had an office on Alvarado Street and plenty of cash. "I hate it when he fucks me," Jan had said. She was now probably saying the same thing about me to him.

Oranges and tomatoes were piled in several crates and apparently were free. I took an orange, bit into the skin and sucked on it. I had exhausted my unemployment benefits since leaving the Sans Hotel.

A guy about forty walked up to me. His hair looked dyed, in fact it didn't look like human hair but more like thread. The hard overhead light shone down on him. He had brown moles on his face, mostly clustered around his mouth. One or two black hairs grew out of each one.

"How you doing?" he asked.

"O.K."

"How'd you like a blow job?"

"No, I don't think so."

"I'm hot, man, I'm excited. I really do it good."

"Listen, I'm sorry, I'm not in the mood."

He walked off angrily. I looked about the large room. There were fifty men waiting. There were ten or twelve state employment clerks sitting at their desks or walking around. They smoked cigarettes and looked more worried than the bums. The clerks were separated from the bums by a heavy wire mesh fence that went from floor to ceiling. Somebody had painted it yellow. It was a very indifferent yellow.

When a clerk had to make a transaction with a bum he unlocked and slid open a small glass window in the wire. When the paperwork was taken care of the clerk would slid the glass window shut, lock it from the inside, and each time it happened, hope seemed to vanish. We all came awake when the window would slide open, any man's chance was our chance, but when it closed, hope evaporated. Then we had each other to look at.

Along the back wall, behind the yellow screen and behind the clerks, were six blackboards. There was white chalk and erasers, just like in grammar school. Five of the blackboards were washed clean, although it was possible to see the ghost of previous messages, of jobs long filled and now lost forever as far as we were concerned.

There was a message on the sixth blackboard:

TOMATO PICKERS WANTED IN BAKERSFIELD

I had thought that machines had put the tomato pickers out of work. Yet, there it was. Humans apparently were less expensive than machines. And machines broke down. Ah.

I looked around the waiting room—there were no Orientals, no Jews, almost no blacks. Most of the bums were poor whites or Chicano. The one or two blacks were already drunk on wine.

157

Now one of the clerks stood up. He was a big man with a beer gut. What you noticed was his yellow shirt with vertical black stripes. The shirt was overstarched, and he wore armbands—to hold up his sleeves like in photographs taken in the 90's. He walked over and unlocked the glass window in the yellow screen.

"All right! There's a truck in back loading up for Bakersfield!"

He slid the window shut, locked it, sat down at his desk and lit a cigarette.

For a moment nobody moved. Then one by one those sitting on the benches began to get up and stretch, their faces expressionless. The men who had been standing dropped their cigarettes on the floor and put them out carefully with the soles of their shoes. Then a slow general exodus began; everyone filed out a side door into a fenced yard.

The sun was coming up. We really looked at each other for the first time. A few men grinned at the sight of a familiar face.

We stood in a line, pushing our way toward the back of the truck, the sun coming up. It was time to get going. We were climbing into a World War II army truck with a high canvas roof, torn. We moved forward, pushing rudely, but at the same time trying to be at least half-polite. Then I got tired of the elbows, I stepped back.

The truck's capacity was admirable. The big Mexican foreman stood to one side at the back of the truck, waving them on in, "All right, all right, let's go, let's go . . ."

The men moved forward slowly, as if into the mouth of the whale.

Through the side of the truck I could see the faces; they were talking quietly and smiling. At the same time I disliked them and felt lonely. Then I decided I could handle tomatoes; I decided to get in. Someone banged into me from behind. It was a fat Mexican woman and she seemed quite emotional. I took her by the hips and boosted her. She was very heavy. She was hard to manage. Finally I got hold of something; it seemed one of my hands had slipped into the deepest recess of her crotch. I boosted her in. Then I reached up to get a grip and pull myself in. I was the last one. The Mexican foreman put his foot on my hand. "No," he said, "we've got enough."

The truck's engine started, stalled, stopped. The driver hit it again. It started and they rolled off.

87

WORKMEN FOR INDUSTRY was located right on the edge of skid row. The bums were better dressed, younger, but just as listless. They sat around on the window ledges, hunched forward, getting warm in the sun and drinking the free coffee that W.F.I. offered. There was no cream and sugar, but it was free. There was no wire partition separating us from the clerks. The telephones rang more often and the clerks were much more relaxed than at the Farm Labor Market.

I walked up to the counter and was given a card and a pen anchored by a chain. "Fill it out," said the clerk, a nice-looking Mexican boy who tried to hid his warmth behind a professional manner.

I began to fill out the card. After address and phone number I wrote: "none." Then after education and work abilities I wrote: "two years L.A. City College. Journalism and Fine Arts."

Then I told the clerk, "I ruined this card. Could I have another?"

He gave me one. I wrote instead: "Graduate, L.A. High School. Shipping clerk, warehouseman, laborer. Some typing."

I handed the card back.

"All right," said the clerk, "sit down and we'll see if anything comes in."

I found a space on a window ledge and sat down. An old black man was sitting next to me. He had an interesting face; he didn't have the usual resigned look that most of us sitting around the room had. He looked as if he was attempting not to laugh at himself and the rest of us.

He saw me glancing at him. He grinned. "Guy who runs this place is sharp. He got fired by the Farm Labor, got pissed, came down here and started this. Specializes in part-time workers. Some guy wants a boxcar unloaded quick and cheap, he calls here."

"Yeah, I've heard."

"Guy needs a boxcar unloaded quick and cheap, he calls here. Guy who runs this place takes 50 per cent. We don't complain. We take what we can get."

"It's O.K. with me. Shit."

"You look down in the mouth. You all right?"

"Lost a woman."

"You'll have others and lose them too."

"Where do they go?"

"Try some of this."

It was a bottle in a bag. I took a hit. Port wine.

"Thanks."

"Ain't no women on skid row."

He passed the bottle to me again. "Don't let him see us drinking. That's the one thing makes him mad."

While we sat drinking several men were called and left for jobs. It cheered us. At least there was some action.

My black friend and I waited, passing the bottle back and forth.

Then it was empty.

"Where's the nearest liquor store?" I asked.

I got the directions and left. Somehow it was always hot on skid row in Los Angeles in the daytime. You'd see old bums walking around in heavy overcoats in the heat. But when the night came down and the Mission was full, those overcoats came in handy.

When I got back from the liquor store my friend was still there.

I sat down and opened the bottle, passed the bag. "Keep it low," he said.

It was comfortable in there drinking the wine.

A few gnats began to gather and circle in front of us. "Wine gnats," he said.

"Sons of bitches are hooked."

"They know what's good."

"They drink to forget their women."

"They just drink."

I waved at them in the air and got one of the wine gnats. When I opened my hand all I could see in my palm was a speck of black and the strange sight of two little wings. Zero.

"Here he comes!"

It was the nice-looking young guy who ran the place. He rushed up to us. "All right! Get out of here! Get the hell out of here, you fuckin' winos! Get the hell out of here before I call the cops!"

He hustled us both to the door, pushing and cursing. I felt guilty, but I felt no anger. Even as he pushed I knew that he didn't really care what we did. He had a large ring on his right hand.

We didn't move fast enough and I caught the ring just over my left eye; I felt the blood start to come and then felt it swell up. My friend and I were back out on the street.

We walked away. We found a doorway and sat on the step. I handed him the bottle. He hit it.

"Good stuff."

He handed me the bottle. I hit it.

"Yeah, good stuff."

"Sun's up."

"Yeah, the sun's up good."

We sat quietly, passing the bottle back and forth. Then the bottle was empty.

"Well," he said, "I gotta be going."

"See you."

He walked off. I got up, went the other way, turned the corner, and walked up Main Street. I went along until I came to the Roxie.

PHOTOS OF the strippers were on display behind the glass out front. I walked up and bought a ticket. The girl in the cage looked better than the photos. Now I had 38 cents left. I walked into the dark theatre eight rows from the front. The first three rows were packed.

I had lucked out. The movie was over and the first stripper was already on. Darlene. The first was usually the worst, an old-timer come down, now reduced to kicking leg in the chorus line most of the time. We had Darlene for openers. Probably someone had been murdered or was on the rag or was having a screaming fit, and this was Darlene's chance to dance solo again.

But Darlene was fine. Skinny, but with breasts. A body like a willow. At the end of that slim back, that slim body, was an enormous behind. It was like a miracle—enough to drive a man crazy.

Darlene was dressed in a long black velvet gown slit very high—her calves and thighs were dead white against the black. She danced and looked out at us through heavily mascaraed eyes. This was her chance. She wanted to come back—to be a featured dancer once again. I was with her. As she worked at the zippers more and more of her began to show, to slip out of that sophisticated black velvet, leg and white flesh. Soon she was down to her pink bra and G-string—the fake diamonds swinging and flashing as she danced.

Darlene danced over and grabbed the stage curtain. The curtain was torn and thick with dust. She grabbed it, dancing to the beat of the four man band and in the light of the pink spotlight.

She began to fuck that curtain. The band rocked in rhythm. Darlene really gave it to that curtain; the band rocked and she rocked. The pink light abruptly switched to purple. The band stepped it up, played all out. She appeared to climax. Her head fell back, her mouth opened.

Then she straightened and danced back to the center of the stage. From where I was sitting I could hear her singing to herself over the music. She took a hold of her pink bra and ripped it off and a guy three rows down lit a cigarette. There was just the G-string now. She pushed her finger into her bellybutton, and moaned.

Darlene remained dancing at stage center. The band was playing very softly. She began a gentle grind. She was fucking us. The beaded G-string was swaying slowly. Then the four man band began to pick up gradually once again. They were reaching for the culmination of the act; the drummer was cracking rim-shots like firecrackers; they looked tired, desperate.

Darlene fingered her naked breasts, showing them to us, her eyes filled with the dream, her lips moist and parted. Then suddenly she turned and waved her enormous behind at us. The beads leaped and flashed, went crazy, sparkled. The spotlight shook and danced like the sun. The four man band crackled and banged. Darlene spun around. She tore away the beads. I looked, they looked. We could see her cunt hairs through the flesh-colored gauze. The band really spanked her ass.

And I couldn't get it up.